Neon Haze

////////

Snakes and Roses

By Chris Sherrit

Chapter 1

Have you ever felt completely exhausted with the world? Dixon Callaway certainly does. A life of sour experiences and painful memories will do that to a man. That and the ridiculous dances he sees before him on this dancefloor. The year is 2109 and Dixon is celebrating this Friday night in much the same way he celebrates most nights. Sitting in the back of a bar or club pickling his brain until he passes out, while watching the rest of the world do its best to keep going. In Denver, Colorado people seem to be trying even more so to hide their own issues. The crippling reality that there is every chance they might get mugged, raped or killed on the way home looms overhead. Dancing like the population of a looney bin broke out and trying to exorcise demons seemed to work for many of these kids. If that didn't - then drinking down the latest alcohol or firing the most popular drugs into their system certainly did the trick. The hangovers and downers the next day would only serve as a swift punch in the face to remind them that their life is still pitiful.

Seated in the darkest corner of this dance club, Dixon takes a large swig from his bottle. Fermented root drinks are not popular, but can be found in a few less than pleasant places, sometimes cropping up in popular venues if you are willing to pay the right price. It doesn't taste nice either, but to Dixon it's strength that he chugs it down for. The almost rhubarb and beetroot taste help draw his attention away from his anger, sadness and continual pain. A pain he has suffered for years now, that heavy emotional suffering that you can force to the side from time to time while you shout at anyone trying to invade on your privacy.

The band performing in the club are thankfully not all that terrible. The bright lights shining out from the musician's costumes are almost all too regular now, as are the holographic instruments being projected before them. A green keytar floats in front of the lead singer as his vocals run through a sparkling mic that pulsates along with him. The guitarist and bassist also motioning away at their instruments, playing them through the haptic gloves they wear which also light up in time with the music. Even the drummer is playing a simulated drum kit, small plastic pads are the only thing real in the cage of neon light that surrounds him. When he finishes a song by smashing the bright yellow cymbals the entire club shoots a rainbow wave of colour through it. The audience is clearly loving it, and Dixon can't help but find himself tapping his foot a little after polishing off another bottle of root booze.

The kids themselves are dressed quite similarly to the band, bright neon colours emanating from their bodies and changing along with the music. It appears quite a few of the people are actual fans of the band in attendance as the band name "Zetsu" warps across their backs.

People always imagine the future being just like all those sci-fi book covers or fancy big budget movies. Well, the future is now and for the most people, it's a big fat dump. As Dixon stumbles out of the club halfway through the band's last song, he bumps into a group of youths. All wearing some variant of what Dixon likes to call "Fuck you!" Oversized leather coats with tribal style designs embroidered and with neon lights built into them, highlighting all of the additions they've made to their apparel.

He notices that they don't seem to have any actual tribal-style tattoos on their skin. Thinking it slightly odd that they seem to be some of the few he's seen lately that haven't had neon tattoos, or even worse holo-tattoo's, embedded into their skin. That's right, holographic displayed tattoo's forced into the skin, running off of the power of the human body - all so that you can say "hey look at how useless I am!" Dixon despised these kinds of people, slightly ironic as he himself fell for the body modding craze when it was picking up heat in his younger years.

He, of course, didn't go for an *in your face* brightly lit tattoo. Body modding, or simply modding, goes far further than the purely aesthetic these days. When he signed up for the Leistung Authoritarian Force there was a mandatory body mod that *had* to be applied. All personnel must be constantly reachable and able to query the LAF database at all times, no exceptions. By that, they meant that you would have to have your phone grafted to your body, and the artificial intelligence switched out for the LAF database AI. Your location and vital statistics were then recorded all day, every day. Dixon had the device grafted to his arm much like most. He wasn't much of a fan of the whole process; large amounts of pain and an everlasting connection to a foreign body were not pleasant thoughts.

No longer working for the LAF, Dixon has had his access to the LAF database removed. "Bout damn time I'm free from that catalogue of horror" Dixon remarks when asked about it. His own irony being that he has now reinstated his old AI, affectionately called "RJ". Being locked away in a digital prison for nearly forty years RJ has altered her attitude. It seems that some of the lines of coding have been burned out by the LAF database and have left a sarcastic asshole in its place, at least in Dixon's words.

"Come on, Dixon, get that old retired ass up," RJ remarks in her custom smooth Irish accent as he slaps at his arm. Dixon falls to the ground trying his best to hold onto the contents of his stomach.

"Yeah, yeah. You want me to rip you out of my arm? Call me a ride home will you?" He says, spitting pre vomit everywhere.

"Rip me out of your arm? That'd be a sight for sore eyes. *Drunk bum savages own arm to shut up phone*, think I've seen that headline already." The dry tone of RJ both insults and amuses Dixon. He smiles pulling himself to his feet. Focusing his eyesight he looks at his forearm seeing the emoji face looking back at him.

"Home, RJ?"

"Home, Dixon!"

Chapter 2

The future of today may not resemble the exciting visions of comics, album covers and filmmakers from the old days, but it certainly has come close. The buildings stand like massive obelisks arranged in odd shapes. Portions of buildings where one would expect to see structure and people working in offices are instead missing. The bright lights of the hover magnets, holding the higher portions of buildings hundreds of feet above the base, highlighting the skyline. Running through those buildings, the hustle and bustle of hover vehicles fly through the gaps. They roll and twist past each other constantly looking like they are on collision paths but avoiding it somehow.

Most people who use transport opt for the automated hover vehicles, some are 'access required' vehicles designed officially for transporting employees. Others are paid transport, mainly focussed on bussing people to specific venues of high importance; business centres and industrial tech-mines. Those who can afford their own hover vehicles tend not to drive them through the city, but instead take the more scenic and safe route around the outside of the city limits. Too high up, however, the poorer masses rarely see any such vehicle in person. The only vehicles seen by them are advertised on the giant building faces showing commercials for the newest model.

Large adverts roll across almost every surface of the buildings up to around two thousand feet. Above that, the towers owned by the rich and powerful glisten in the light. The adverts ranging from a variety of products from body modifications to robotic house appliances to the latest action movie coming this summer. News reports are broadcast on certain buildings at every hour of the day. Almost plastic looking faces that pose an inhuman smile inform the cities of the daily horrors and tragedies, making sure to put extra emphasis on any new merger or corporate move. The most common commercial seen around the city buildings are Halos pride and joy.

The company, which came into existence around two hundred years ago, the first to have the idea of providing the world with a long line of non-lethal alternatives to weapons. Wanting to make the world use "zero rounds" of ammunition being their goal, hence the original branding of Zero Round Industries. ZR for short. After having only small success but large amounts of investments from rich liberal sources, they branched out to try and tackle humanities weaknesses. In the early twenty-first century, they struck gold, a discovery that within every person's genes was a set of testable qualities that would allow the potential success of a person to be known. Taking the chance to rebrand themselves at this point to Halo Industries, perhaps to get a fresh slate with the public, perhaps to avoid the ironic holes in naming themselves Zero Round. Overnight the media went into a tornado of excitement, broadcasting around the globe that they could now predict how rich you would be, or how powerful. Of course, an exact profession could never be predicted from the genes, but to a quite impressive degree of accuracy, it worked. Becoming known as getting Gene Identified, then "Gene ID'd" and now more commonly just called an individual's "GID".

Society changed very quickly after that. The sceptics continued to try and find evidence of foul play in the research or fabricated documents and results. Even with the investigation into what they thought was impossible, those non-believers still had themselves tested. After finding out that they were all within the mid to high-level GIDs, they quietened down.

The high-level GIDs went on a yearlong celebration, patting themselves on the back for being born into their lifestyles. As a result, companies changed and there were fewer attempts to try and employ in a politically correct fashion. Now companies simply pick the best of the applicants, nobody argues that it's unfair. Why would you?

The low-level GIDs did an international shoulder shrug and tried their best to get on with things, ignoring the high levels as they went about their day to day trivial jobs. Appreciating that they hadn't really achieved much in their life up to this point, the low levels didn't have much ambition to try and push themselves towards anything in the future. There was no need for them to cause a giant fuss. It was now scientifically proven that they were in the right place. That notion came as a comfort to some - that they weren't losing out on being their best self.

The elite GIDs were those who were already living at the top of the food chain. The company CEO's and world leaders, their high scores were what initially drew the sceptics to question everything. It was a little ironic that those earning the most were predicted to earn the most, like they had paid to have this result. Rather than irony, this was just proving the point that their GID scores were correct.

All of the elites would react in the same way when they found out their results. Pretending to sit cool and calm in their boardrooms, they would wait patiently for the envelope to arrive. Upon opening it - their faces would pull an arrogant "I knew all along" - you could see the bead of sweat that rolled down their brow. They had confidence in themselves but there was the thought at the back of their heads that they may be useless.

 Prior to the discovery of the gene, the world has taken a very aggressive turn towards a corporate approach. Although the past would claim that corporations own everything and dictate the governments. Nowadays the corporations *are* the governments, the result of histories "Corporate wars".

 Three years into a war that had broken out between the United States and China, a spies report to the US president of China's technological superiority rumbled many fears. It was suspected that hackers had been posing as Russian nationals who were interfering in American companies and political elections. The suspicion of Russia brought fourth several strikes on Russian territories. China chortled as the two took strikes at each other. They never knew that Russia had in fact been hacking into their systems, and while sending forces to meet the American onslaught they took Chinese territory at a speedy rate. After Britain's departure from the European Union, the EU banded together and united fully under one banner, seeking to take the island back during the chaos.

 In the year 2035, amidst all this, a dictator by the name of Tristan Moreno managed to rise to power in Argentina. A decorated general with a mean streak a hundred miles wide, and a level of focus that appeared unmatched, he took control of the country through force and was met with a high level of support initially. The people of Argentina felt their government was simply a collection of powerful men trying to line their pockets rather than improve the quality of life for everyone. Moreno's eyes bulged with the amount of power he had taken on, putting military personnel in the highest levels of government and changing the constitution to better suit his intentions.

Not one for thinking his political moves that far ahead, he quickly crashed the Argentinian economy. The currency fell to an all-time low and the population of most countries found that their yearly salary would be able to buy out Argentinian companies and property with change to spare. The changes that had been made didn't stop or slow anyone from doing this either, they sped up the process in fact. Several of the larger industrial companies saw an opportunity and took a firm grasp of it. The oil and energy giant Leistung managed to take ownership of the most land and best property. The oil and energy contracts outstanding with all the normally functioning countries, provided a steady level of cash flow for them to build huge production plants around the airports, military bases and naval bases.

With Leistung controlling so much, General Moreno had to create contracts with them to try and keep control. Again, his bold changes to the constitution ended up biting him, as the company used loopholes to their advantage. The bulk of the land that they had bought but weren't using was farmland, and this turned the people against General Moreno in a demand for change. Leistung stepped in to provide help with the stockpile of supplies they had accumulated in their properties. Fast building the image that they were a company who was on the *everyday man's* side their popularity grew. Teams of the military began to convert to Leistung and became corporate mercenaries. This led to the total take-over of the country by a corporation. The general, having cut ties to all other countries when he came to power and insulting almost every world leader, only helped the company in their coup.

Having taken one country, Leistung began its move towards putting pressure on the neighbours around them. South America grinded to a halt as they tried to reason with this new entity. One by one countries began to fall and join Leistung in some of the largest "mergers and acquisitions" anyone had seen. In response to South America now being almost rebranded, other countries began to take action.

Still spit-taking in disbelief, the USA and parts of the EU began forcing sanctions on the company and the business ventures they had outside of their new country. By this point it didn't matter, the company replied in a guffaw - that the sanctions would be met with a far stricter show of action. All the production plants of North American and European countries within the Leistung republic would no longer be able to function, or would be forced out of ownership and re-purposed to their objectives.

Rival businesses began to go into hysterical panic as they tried to put weight on governments to either pull away from fighting Leistung, or push them further into shutting them down. Potential political investors held the largest megaphones and governments followed their orders. North America pulled back and allowed several EU countries to take the hit as they pushed against this bully.

With an understandable arrogance in themselves, troops were flown into the Leistung Republic, only to discover that this was an entire continent being run by the company. They were outnumbered massively, and with the pushes in technology Leistung had managed to carry out with all the resources they were dreadfully outgunned as well. The attempted battles only resulted in mass panic around Europe. At this point the loop of corporations pressuring governments and countries into changing leadership really took off. Leistung already had South America, Praetorium took control of Europe and parts of Africa. The rest of Africa along with Australia fell to Coracle, Fenghuang was eagerly waiting to rip through Asia, expanding out of China to take Japan and Russia. The USA and Canada were the last to tumble and surrendered to Zero Round.

With that, the CEOs of these companies became the world leaders. With fewer voices to listen to and consider, the group formed a council that met on certain occasions to discuss "potential business". Righting the wrongs they thought the world had, but only creating new ones in their place. Buildings got taller and taller, business got faster and faster and everyone stuck in between struggled to keep up. Certain companies brokered "peace deals" in order to try and solidify their territories. The LAF for example, partially a police force, partially mercenaries owned by Leistung, rented out a few spots across America in a deal with Zero Round. They, in turn, provided some factory space for Leistung to speed up their production line.

Denver was one of the few places with a strong presence from more than one or two super corporations. Fenghuang also has several buildings being rented out from Zero Round. Giving them the presence to create jobs and promote their product to more people, bullshit! The gangs of the city all knowing that if they can't get hold of a black market weapon from a desperate ZR employee they can always go to Fenghuang for some prime chaos creators. This is more than likely the true purpose of Fenghuang's presence, to create disorder amongst the people and confusion throughout those who would control.

It was no wonder that the low levellers did not rise up when everyone got their GID - they were still trying to figure out where they were going to get food for that week. As you would expect crime has risen in the low-level neighbourhoods, gangs execute their own justice and control on small regions at ground level. Some of them striking "sponsorships" from corporate bigwigs, only so they can get some cheap protection while they organise shady dealings.

Dixon himself holds a fairly average score. While becoming a gang member at a low-level GID might be considered doing well for yourself - getting employed under the LAF was also doing well for himself. Although he only really operated at an officer's level while part of the force - he attempted to rise to the rank of detective but was denied. Only a small number of mid levellers have made it to detective, they still aren't assigned high-value cases though. After the accident, Dixon decided that he'd had enough of taking orders from self-centred pricks and young up and comers. His training and experience had led him into "the lows" before, missing person statements, assaults, rapes, everything under the sun. Almost always there was a corpse to deal with, seeing another dead abused woman or child caught in crossfire chipped away at Dixon every time he saw one.

He still returns to the lows these days, but only when his drunken desperation gets the better of him. Ending up in a broken down building paying a stripper for an hour of her time before the emotions hidden inside him break out. Most of his drunk encounters in the low ended being thrown out by a meathead bouncer, tweaking off of some morbidly named drug cocktail.

Although RJ may give him a hard time quite a bit, it is also in her interests to make sure that he stays alive. Without the power of his body, she would die out within a few days. There's a chance that her AI could be removed from Dixon and brought back to life. The places he ends up passing out or getting in trouble, it would be far more likely that his body would be torn apart or reduced to nothing.

Chapter 3

It was that day of the year again for Dixon. The day that he never wanted to come, but every time it came around his head was numbed from reality with memories that almost made him feel human.

Standing in the cemetery in front of his daughters' graves the rain beat down on him. He barely felt the cold damp working deeper into his clothes, not because he was drunk but because he could only feel his little girls.

Jenny's grave had a wreath propped up against it, the flowers bright and fresh, he hadn't put the wreath there. He'd set the small stuffed snake toy next to it. It wilted a little as the moisture ran through the soft material.

Rose's grave also had a wreath propped on it. Beautiful roses in a circle highlighting her name on the gravestone. Dixon's single rose sitting on the ground braced against the wreath.

A funeral party walk by, all dressed in the standard black, a few covering their faces as they wept walking past. Their hats covering them from the rain, their tears visibly glinting in the light. Nobody could tell if Dixon cried from the drops of water running down his face. He shed several tears as he looked at two place markers stuck in the mud to show he'd lost his family.

"Come on, Dixon, you'll catch a cold standing in this rain" RJ's voice said, muffled a little from his sleeve.

Turning to walk from the graves, he muddles into the funeral party crowd. Reaching into his coat as he watches his feet carry him forward. Pulling a bottle from his coat - he pops the cork. Forgetting what spirit he'd chosen to drown himself in this time he throws it back. The burning sensation warming his insides, but not numbing the cold hurt in his heart.

Stumbling home, Dixon ignores the prostitute's offers, the youth's empty threats. A gang of guys try to approach him but, turn back as he spots them, smashing the bottle on the wall and staring them down.

RJ intervenes before Dixon takes things further. "Dixon, please get us home. You'll only make yourself dumber mixing in with that crowd."

"I wasn't making friends, RJ" Dixon murmurs between hiccups.

"Oh really? You look like you're a good match for them", her voice jabbing.

"Fuck you, RJ."

"Love you too, Dixon."

Reaching his door he tosses the broken bottle. Tripping in the door he crawls to his feet again and slumps into his bed, passing out.

Waking up with blurred vision and a pulsating echo of pain in his head, Dixon opens his eyes.

"Hey buddy, come on man, wake up!"

Dixon rolled out of his bed, a stale smell in the air, possibly his own vomit or piss on the bed? He couldn't distinguish the difference.

"Jimmy?" He said to the silhouette figure before him.

"Yeah buddy, it's me. You trying to fill that head with booze again and pickle your brain?" Jimmy leaned against the doorframe.

"So what's it to you?" Dixon scratched his head, blinking several times to try and clear his vision.

"Well nobody wants to hold onto your brain" Turning from the doorway, Jimmy walks to the kitchen and pours two mugs of coffee.

"Nobody seems to want your brain either, pretty boy" RJ quips.

"Morning RJ," Jimmy says sarcastically.

Rising from his bed and seeing the pool of liquid and chunks he was lying, in Dixon then tastes the remains in his mouth. It was indeed vomit he was smelling. Tossing on a shirt, he walks through to the kitchen and takes the coffee from Jimmy.

"Hey, thank you and fuck you" Retorting in disgust - Dixon sips at the coffee. Whipping open the cupboard and rifling through its contents.

"What? Not sweet enough" Jimmy laughs while taking a seat. Dixon pushes his hand deeper into the cupboard and pulls out a bottle of whisky, popping the bottle cap off and pouring it into his mug. Sipping at his drink again he closes his eyes and sighs.

"Better?" Jimmy says, while visibly showing concern.

"Better!" replies Dixon, as he flumps down into the seat opposite Jimmy.

"You are a real fucking mess, Dix" says Jimmy.

"Yeah? And you're here for some fucking reason, Kersh" staring harshly at Jimmy. He doesn't hate him but with the level of hangover he has right now, Dixon certainly didn't feel like having a chat.

"I'm just checking up on you buddy!" The Boston accent creeping through Jimmy's apprehension made him sound like he was being cheeky sometimes, Dixon couldn't help but like that.

Jimmy Kershon or "Kersh", as Dixon nicknamed him, also worked for the LAF. The two were partners for nearly twenty-five years and had ended up in almost a movie like buddy cop friendship. Dixon being the pessimistic hard-edged one of the group, Jimmy was quite the opposite. A happy-faced pleasant person to be around. Two years younger than Dixon although most would assume they were ten years apart. Jimmy was a handsome guy who did his best to keep himself well-groomed, and also keep a masculine but welcoming appearance. "Pretty boys don't get respect in the force!" he'd say after locking up another young punk who took a swing at him for thinking he was soft.

Dixon used to look like a man not to be messed with, and for the most part, his broad shoulders and large presence still gave off that impression. The dried in vomit in his now scruffy beard, and sweaty unkempt hair, made him look worthless. He stank like he hadn't washed in a month, not that he could remember the last time he'd cleaned. Jimmy didn't want to start poking too much fun at his look though. He was his best friend after all, his only friend. After the accident Jimmy took Dixon in. There was no way he was going to let the man who'd saved his life countless times fall into the gutter.

Another reason Jimmy wanted to help his friend was that he considered him almost like family. Dixon had been married to a beautiful woman and they had two daughters, Rose and Jenny. He would regularly look at their photo in Dixon's apartment when he visited. Two gorgeous young girls who were taken far too young. There were no photos of the ex-wife, Sadie, to be seen in the living room.

Jimmy had helped care for the kids, frequently sitting for them when Dixon and his wife would go off on trips or go out for date night. He loved being called Uncle Jimmy, he always wanted kids of his own when he settled down with a bride. When the crash happened and Dixon was pulled from the wreckage along with his wife, he was screaming in fury. Even when the surgeons were operating on his arm he screamed in anger at the idiot who collided with them.

Both girls died in the car, their bodies broken and burned too badly for an open casket funeral. It was shortly after this that the divorce pushed Dixon over the edge and Jimmy was there to catch him. RJ had almost taken on the role of proxy amalgamation of both Dixon's daughters. Rose's kind intention teamed with Jenny's sharp wit. Jimmy could almost picture a teenage daughter of Dixon's with her mother's intelligence and her father's ferocity.

"Want to grab some breakfast? I'm buying" Jimmy looked at the rose and snake tattoo on Dixon's arm, intertwined around each other and covering the large scar up his arm. Jimmy knew that the tattoo was for his daughters, the two of them loved going to the zoo, and Jenny would always race to the reptile enclosures to see the snakes. He liked his partner's tattoo but also felt a little bit of pain every time he saw it.

"You're buying? I guess I have to come now" Dixon threw back the rest of his drink, stood up and marched for the door.

"Dixon?" RJ enquires.

"Uh, hey Dix?" Jimmy called. Dixon turning to see what was holding him up.

"Dixon?" RJ enquires again.

"Might want to put on some clothes. I don't want to arrest you for indecent exposure" Jimmy cocks his head at Dixon's lower half. Looking down, Dixon remembers that he's only wearing his vomit covered boxers and a shirt with a picture of a man lying face surrounded by bottles of beer and the caption "Fit Shaced".

"Guess you're right" Dixon replies with a look that could be his bleary-eyed hangover or could be a bit of the irritation he's feeling.

"This the most action you've had in a while, Jimmy?" RJ remarks.

"I'll meet you at the car," Jimmy says as he slips out the door.

When Dixon finally appears and collapses into the passenger seat Jimmy rolls his eyes and starts the engine. Pulling away in the LAF issued detectives car, the radio murmurs in the background, all the callouts of crimes in progress. Jimmy was proud of his car, being one of the few mid levellers to make it to detective made him feel distinctive. Regularly washing his car, it was one of the few that didn't have graffiti along the side of it reading "LAFfing stock".

Dixon looked out at the streets as they passed by. Prostitutes and drug dealers on most corners talking to anyone walking by. Children playing games using drones as Frisbees or kicking around garbage in slum soccer. It didn't make him happy to see the kids have to grow up in a place like this. He felt the most pain knowing that their parents were probably the drug dealers or prostitutes standing nearby. Either that or their parents were due money to them.

Jimmy pulled the car into a local diner about ten miles from Dixon's place, four miles from the LAF headquarters. It was the diner they used to get breakfast most mornings when they worked together. Dixon hadn't been here for several years.

"Wow, Momma's Bistro" Dixon stepped out of the car and looks at the large sign blinking on top of the diner. "Does momma still work here?"

"What? Of course not. She died like six years ago" Jimmy remarked as he held the door open for Dixon. Several LAF cops sitting having their own breakfast nod to Jimmy as they take a booth. Dixon catching the eyes of a few younger officers, their curiosity quite evident.

They ordered their standard breakfast, a stack of pancakes each, bacon, eggs, sausages, blood pudding and about enough coffee to put a meth addict at ease. Jimmy didn't have as much of the coffee, of course, it perked Dixon up though.

Seeing the life beginning to pour back into Dixon, Jimmy leaned over the table and whispers "I got something for you" with a hint of excitement.

"Is it a date?" RJ jokes, Jimmy looks at Dixon's arm and then back.

"What?" Dixons face pinching in confusion.

"I got something for you. I got a call last night of a disturbance in an apartment. Think you're going to want to come along with me" Jimmy's face lighting up as he talked.

"Why? Whose apartment is it? Not like I could do anything anyway, I'm not one of you anymore, Kersh!" Dixon stared back, an eyebrow raised.

"Oh, I think you'll be interested…" Jimmy looked around the diner to make sure nobody was paying attention.

"It's Chester Lopez's place!"

Chapter 4

As they pulled up to the mega high rise building Dixon couldn't help but look up and try to take in just how tall it was. Blinded by the sun that singes the remains of his hangover, he looked at Jimmy.

"He lives here?" Pointing to the building as Jimmy reached for the door handle.

"Looks expensive, he must be doing well for himself," says RJ.

"Promoted twice since we last saw him, RJ." Jimmy looks up to Dixon. "You think I just brought you to a fancy building to show you how nice the shitter was?" Jimmy flashed his cheeky grin, Dixon smirked and followed him inside.

"Be serious, you've done that before haven't you, J-Kersh?" says RJ.

"I told you, stop calling me that RJ." Jimmy grunts.

"So it's a domestic disturbance, what? Music too loud?" Dixon asked.

"Apparently there were reports of loud crashes and bangs, shouting and a female screaming" Jimmy said as the two of them walked past the reception desk. Flashing his badge at the pretty girl behind the desk, it illuminates projecting out about an inch. They enter the lift to take them to the eighty-second floor.

"You think it's really a good idea bringing me here?" Dixon asks - crunching his fists thinking of seeing his enemy.

"Well, I'm here to question him about the disturbance last night. You're going to wait outside. Maybe I'll call you in for a chat, maybe I won't" Jimmy winked at Dixon as the lift picks up speed.

They arrive at the eighty-second floor and walk down the corridor. The hallway is dimly lit like it was a seedy underground club. The décor contrasting with a super professional business feel. They walk around several corners before finally coming to the right door.

"827 D, this is it. Are you going to be ok?" Jimmy asks Dixon with a vague look of concern on his face.

"Me? Peachy!" Dixon knocks on the door hard and steps back, crossing his hands together behind his back.

"If peaches were likely to violently explode, maybe," RJ says, Dixon taps his arm and mute's RJ.

The door opens with the sound of pounding music, the smell of something stale and unnatural, and a medium sized man with large hair.

"Uh, yes, can I help you?" the irritated face questions.

"Mr Lopez?" Jimmy crosses his hands and lowers his head, game face on.

"Who the fuck wants to know" Clearly a good foot shorter than the two of them, the man tries to intimidate them by opening the door a little further. His striped suit screaming his GID level, and the Fenghuang logo on the chest confirming just how high levelled he is.

"Detective Kershon, this is Dixon Callaway" Flashing his badge again Jimmy lets the man investigate the holographic projection of his badge. "I'm guessing you are Mr Lopez then?"

"Uh yes, sorry detective, what is the issue?" The arrogant grimace on Chester's face drops.

"There was a disturbance reported in the building last night, just wanted to come in and ask you a few questions if that's alright, sir?" Jimmy slips the badge back into his jacket pocket. Chester steps back, holding the door open allowing them to enter, locking eyes with Dixon as he passes. Dixon's rage only just being held at bay as he enters. Chester clearly recognizes him but doesn't know from where, this only angering Dixon further.

As they look around the apartment Dixon's hate turns to disgust at the amount of space he sees before him. A large open plan living room, kitchen and games area are framed by giant windows that look out over the city. From up here it almost looks quite nice. A staircase pokes out of the far wall. Dixon's eyes follow them up as he realises that there is an entire top floor to the apartment comprised of an office and gigantic master bedroom.

"Pretty sweet, huh?" Chester boasts, walking past and sitting down on the sofa, resting his feet on the black coffee table in front of him. Jimmy can't help but try to figure out what it is holding up his hair while he looks around; product, misshaped skull or some strangely hidden scaffolding?

"Was there anyone here last night with you?" Jimmy brings up his arm, the LAF database springing to life and projecting from the screen grafted to him.

"Oh yes, I had a, um....friend here" Chester removes his feet from the table and sits up as he tries to hide the obvious.

"A friend huh?" A smile creeps across Jimmy's face. Dixon meanwhile, is slowly wandering around the apartment, Chester occasionally looking at him, curious where he's wandering.

Looking around the kitchen, there are knocked over glasses and mugs that Dixon notices. Far too many for just two people. He ascends the staircase while Jimmy enquires further.

"Don't mind him. He's just making sure everything is alright in the apartment. Now, there were reports of a woman screaming - was this your.....friend?" Jimmy raises an eyebrow.

"Um, no, we were watching a horror movie" Chester's jaw shifting, he's lying, that part is obvious. Jimmy wonders how he's managed to make it so far in Fenghuang. The guys over there are ruthless business types. Probably the son of some executive.

"Looks like it was a horror movie up here" Dixon shouts down as he approaches the bedroom window, looking down into the living room, holding up white and black thongs on each index finger. One of the thongs is splattered with blood around the waistband. Dixon smiles down to Jimmy, who in turn looks at Chester while crossing his arms.

"Just the one friend was it?" Jimmy asks

His head drops and Chester sighs loudly. "Ok yeah, I had some hookers back here. So what? That isn't illegal detective!" He raises his arms in argument.

"No, one of those pieces of underwear looked like it had blood on it though, care to explain?" Jimmy nods to Dixon who continues searching around.

Leaving the bedroom he gently pushes open the office door. It's set out like an old study, many books line the walls, or at least the illusion of books. Dixon running his hand along the spines and discovers that they are all one piece. This guy may be a high-level prick, but he certainly has some cheap taste. Scattered on the desk are little statuettes of people, each of them appearing to represent a different class. The lower GID statuettes wearing raggedy clothing, the mid-level GID's wearing everything from a regular shirt and trousers to gang-affiliated apparel. The high GID's have suits and exuberant outfits and stand in egotistical poses.

A group of papers pour out of a folder onto the desk, drawing Dixon's eyes, he realises he can't remember the last time he saw physical paper. Written across the front of the folder are the words CONFIDENTIAL! FOR AUTHORISED EYES ONLY. Dixon's eyes perk up, like seeing this has brought him back to his old LAF force days. He flicks open the cover and sees a long document headed with two company names. Fenghuang and Zero Round. The text reading in long legal terms of a merger between the two. Flipping one of the pages Dixon's eyes widen even further as he sees a large bold piece of text.

'Step 2. *Reconstruct GID hierarchy*' heads several paragraphs as Dixon skims over. His fists crunch again as he reads further.

"Hey, you can't read that!" Chester bursts in the room and musters the papers and folder together.

"Paper huh? Wow, I haven't seen that shit in decades" Jimmy slowly sways into the room following Chester. "Dixon? We're done here!" Dixon grinds his teeth as he walks out of the office, unsure how to process the words he saw in the document.

"You guys aren't even high GID's are you? Keep your filthy fucking hands off my stuff and get out." His voice grinds at Dixon, stopping him in his tracks. He'd almost forgotten who Chester was, turning he reveals the terrifying lowered brow that used to bring gang members ego down to size.

"March eighteenth, twenty-two eighty. Ring a bell?" Dixon slowly walks back into the office, Jimmy leans in the doorway as the misplaced self-importance drops from Chester's face.

"No, no, no way!" The colour also drains from Chester's face, his lips quivering and body tensing up.

"You leave a club with some rancid hooker and drive around like a maniac, all jacked up on god knows how many substances." Dixon towers over Chester as he recites the events of the night that brings him so much pain.

"Didn't quite make it home in one piece though did you?" Dixon grabs Chester's collar, lifting him from the ground up to his eye line.

"You can't do this to me. You're just low GID's!" Chester splutters out through his rising fear.

"Yeah? Who the fuck cares?" Dixon tosses Chester over his desk with alarming ease. Jimmy looks on surprised, he thought his former partner would have lost his strength with all the drinking and destroying himself.

Crashing over the top of the desk and into a pile on the floor, Chester quickly tries to gather himself, pulling the papers back while looking up in anger.

"You two are going to fucking pay for this. Do you have any idea who the fuck I am?" Chester spits at Dixon who circles around the desk towards him.

"You're the dumb fuck that got loaded and killed my daughters!" Standing over the pile of bile, Dixon's fists crack again. Swiftly plugging a foot into Chester's chest he is launched three feet over the room. Wasting no time Dixon then picks him up by the collar, growling as he drags him back to his desk. Chester coughs hard, trying to gasp back air into his lungs before the sledgehammer of Dixon's fist collides with his face. Blood seeps from his broken lip long before the surge of pain fills his cheek. Dixon pummels his face again and again and again, Jimmy looks on with folded arms.

"Ok that's enough, Dix" Jimmy shouts as Dixon reels his arm back again. The blood drips from Chester's face in large clumps onto the cream carpet. Jimmy knows it can't go too far, but also wants to give this worthless sack of skin to his friend to try and bring some kind of closure. It probably wouldn't work for Dixon, it would perhaps work for Jimmy.

Dixon looks back at Jimmy, his chest heaving as his whole body aches with rage. He closes his grip around Chester's collar as he spits blood and tries to open his now swollen eye. Dixon grits his teeth as he suddenly slams Chester's head against the edge of the desk. An audible crunch and yelp can be heard as he hits the ground unconscious. Dixon turns from his victim and exits the office. Jimmy can't help but notice that he doesn't seem to be blinking at all.

Pressing two fingers to Chester's neck, he confirms he is still alive and brings up the LAF database on his arm.

"HQ? This is Detective Kershon, I'm at the disturbance report at 827 D Yomi heights." There are some bleeps and chattering noises from his arm and a voice replies.

"Confirmed, what is your status, detective?" The AI voice replies in a clear American accent.

"Yeah, the uh, occupant of the residence was non-cooperative. Had to use force, please send immediate medical support." Jimmy watches a small dribble of blood seeps out of Chester's mouth.

A couple of beeps and a whirr later, "Confirmed, medics on route." Jimmy lowers his arm, the display blinking off. As Jimmy leaves the office and the apartment, he finds Dixon standing in the corridor, almost idling as the door closes Jimmy leans around him.

"You ok buddy?" asks Jimmy

"Yeah, I'm fine" Dixon finally blinks and lowers his head, looking around and eventually catching Jimmy's eyes. "I'm fine buddy, thanks. I just don't know how to feel".

"I'm not surprised. I still don't know if I want to go back there and finish him off!" Jimmy spreads a smirk as he pats Dixon's shoulder.

"He's still alive? I kind of blacked out there." says Dixon as the two of them leave the building. Jimmy nodding at the receptionist as they pass, she smiles flirtatiously back before seeing the blood dripping from Dixon's hands and sharply gasps.

Chapter 5

Dropping Dixon off at his home, Jimmy rolls down the window and shouts out, "I'll come back around tonight. We'll have some beers or split a bottle of whiskey, yeah?" Jimmy watches his friend shuffle up the steps to the door, not looking Dixon waves a hand back.

Was it the best thing for the prick to be confronted like that? Should it have been the victim's father that confronted him? Jimmy pondered if justice today was really just people getting revenge. This time it certainly felt like it.

Dixon opens his apartment door and instantly grabbed the bottle that had been left on the counter top. Closing the door he gulped down three large swigs of booze before his eyes lock on something. He stops, taking the bottle from his lips and stumbling forward to the picture of his two little girls in the frame on the wall. Picking it gently from the hook, he holds it close, his eyes beginning to well up as the happiest memories of his life pour back into his head.

He hasn't been able to think of his family in that kind of setting since it all happened. Falling into his chair his eyes look over their hair, their friendly eyes and honest smiles. A small smile emerging amongst the tears, he thinks out loud to himself, "I got him, girls, I got him, you're going to be okay now."

Taking a large breath he sighs, a warm feeling grows in his chest as the love for his daughters begins to overtake the intense hatred and pain. Putting the bottle down next to his chair he lifts his arm up. Running his other hand over the tattoo covering his scar, he can still feel the remains of his injury, but now sees beauty in what covers his skin. Running his fingers down the snake's body followed by the rose he lets out a small chuckle.

"You can rest now, girls," Dixon says with a closed lip smile. It is not the girls who can rest now, they are already. It is Dixon who can now rest. With that he relaxes in his chair, slowly closing his eyes and drifting off to sleep. A rest his mind and body have needed since the crash unfolds some of the stresses in Dixon and he begins to dream.

Sitting on their favourite beach Dixon and Sadie watch as their girls play and splash in the water. Their innocent laughter drifting across the air as Sadie leans into Dixon's chest, resting her head on him. They watch the girls play in joy as the sun seems to roll perceptibly across the sky, disappearing behind the horizon - the moon then follows after it. The sky lit up like a laser show as the beach is cast in a calming dull white light. Dixon leans in to kiss his wife's head as suddenly there is a bright white flash.

The desk in Chester's office flickers into view, and then the folder containing the documents. The cover of the folder flips open and before the text can be read the papers turn a dark red colour. Blood begins to trickle out of the paper creating a larger and larger puddle on the desktop. Eventually pouring off the desk as the whole vision begins to drift off into darkness, in turn, a group of screams grow in volume. People crying out in anguish, begging for help, some angrily screaming. The screams grow larger and larger until they cut out altogether.

A single scream directly in Dixon's ear jolts him awake. He springs forward in his seat accidentally knocking over the bottle sitting next to it. He picks it up in a panicked fumble, putting it on the counter and breathing heavily. Sweat pours from his forehead as he struggles to realise what just happened. He must have been dreaming, that much he could figure out. What was the end of his dream about though? Dixon's memory then reminds him of the encounter in the office. The folder with the legal documents, looking over the mention of the merger and the reconstruction of the GID's hierarchy. As his memory blinks over the image of the pyramid with the heading "old", the clear distinction of Low-level, Mid-level, High-level, Executive and Council depicted inside it. A smaller pyramid is displayed below it with "new" written above it. There are fewer contents in this one, Low-level, High-level and Council. As Dixon recalls this the screams of his dream bounce around as well.

Calming himself as he processes the information, he picks up the cap for the bottle and screws it on tight. Putting it back in the cupboard and looking around his apartment.

"Welcome back sleepy head," RJ says.

"What happened?" asks Dixon.

"You passed out, and for once it wasn't from booze. You've needed that in I don't know *how* long." RJ's voice sounding slightly relieved as Dixon stands up.

"Shit! What a crap heap." Taking in the amount of neglect he'd given his living space, he thought it a little strange that Jimmy hadn't mentioned anything when he'd visited. He flicks the switch for the blinds and the slats of metal begin to shift off the windows. The light revealing more abandonment, Dixon slowly begins to realise just how bad he'd let himself sink. Jimmy probably didn't say anything because he didn't want to make things worse. There was also the possibility that Jimmy had tried to say something, but Dixon had hit rock bottom too hard to pay attention.

Dixon couldn't remember much of what happened after his divorce. Most of it was a drunken blur covered in a vomit and piss haze. He raises his arm and presses the display.

"RJ?" he asks.

"What's up? I'm not ordering you more booze. Oh and don't mute me again!" She replies with a hint of distaste.

"Oh come on RJ, I couldn't have you ripping the crap out of that hairpiece."

"He was a real fucking hairpiece" RJ cracks.

"Is this seriously how my place has been all these years?" Dixon says in realisation.

"This shit sty? Yeah, this is your home. I tried to get you to clean it, you switched me off for three days." Says RJ

"I did?" Raising an eyebrow Dixon begins to pick up some of the dirty clothes sitting around.

"Yup" she pops in reply "Dick!"

Dixon stops and looks at his arm, holding a ball of clothes he didn't even know he'd bought. A straight mouthed emoji stares back at him.

"Ok, I'm sorry, guess I've been a little fucked up. Not exactly like my life has played out like a fairy-tale." He opens the large metal washing machine, its squeaking hinges screaming out with lack of use. Closing the lid, he looks for a button to press, the display on the front of the machine flickering before displaying the message "Wash cycle – Heavy duty". Dixon smirks and tilts his head.

"Turning a new page are we?" RJ asks.

"I don't know if you saw everything that went down with that dick barnacle, Chester Lopez, but I just had the craziest dream." Dixon slams the lid closed after pouring in various cleaning liquids.

"Your brain was going wild. Lighting up like a firework display" RJ sounds curious.

"It's strange, I can remember it quite vividly, RJ. Feel like I should still be trying to figure out if what I did to Chester was right or wrong." He presses a few lights on the machine and it clunks and shakes to life.

"The dick barnacle?"

"Yeah, seeing that sack bleed was good. Those documents are still in my head though. They are going to try and push even more people into low-level GIDs. What good is that going to do?" Dixon says while pulling an unopened box of kitchen cloths.

"Maybe they are wanting to simplify things?" RJ suggests.

"Yeah, maybe. That's a scary thought though. People trying to simplify things for the rest of us is going to go wrong somewhere, right?" Dixon finds a bottle of cleaning liquid with a note stuck to it. USE! With a winking face and Jimmy's initials below it. He had attempted to get Dixon to clean in his own subtle way.

"Sometimes people need things simple, but these Feng guys? They've always seemed like a shady group to me, Dix" when RJ used his name Dixon always paid close attention.

Fenghuang was renowned for their success, commercials sprawling over buildings with reviews of their products. Six-star kitchen appliances, the best vacation locations, new and improved body mods. Dixon never understood why they added the extra star to their ratings.

Regardless of all the press they received, everyone knew the rumours. People being tossed off of buildings by executives displeased with their department's staff. Fenghuang muscle, also known as "talons", had been seen savagely beating people in alleyways, allegedly because they'd bad mouthed the executive levels of the company. The bright yellow highlighting the outline of their yakuza style tattoos. Many of them wearing shirts with the backs removed to reveal the tattoos. Large Chinese phoenix birds beaming in colour, their feathers a fine glowing red. The helmets they wore - a black phoenix head with glowing yellow eyes. Ruthless creatures.

"Fuck," Dixon says brooding over the consequences of the situation.

"What are you going to do?" RJ's voice seeming more curious than before.

"I've got to speak to Kersh!"

Chapter 6

Jimmy exits his car, pulling the bag of booze from the passenger's footwell. The local kids run past him with their augmented reality helmets, looks like their playing some sort of laser tag style game. The noises from their helmets a pleasant change from the normal screaming and anger he's used to dealing with on the job.

As he walks into the building he sees that the out of order sign on the elevator is still there. The dirt and dust around the frame building up further every time he's here. He sighs and turns to the stairwell, counting the number of needles and drug inhalers he sees on the way up. There are a couple more than the last time he was here. There's still a collection of questionable delinquents in this block.

Knocking on Dixon's door he listens out for the normal bang of Dixon rolling off the bed or sofa with a bottle. Not hearing anything, he assumes that he's passed out, reaching for the door handle it suddenly swings open.

Jimmy jitters and blinks several times at the sight before him. A tall clean-shaven man, washed and smelling quite pleasant, wearing a neat button up shirt and jeans. Numerous seconds pass before he realises its Dixon.

"Kersh, come on in" Dixon stands aside, Jimmy slowly enters. Looking back at Dixon as he walks into the apartment, he doesn't even notice the change in the surroundings

"Hey, uh, buddy. Feeling better?" Jimmy musters a smile and hands the bag of booze to Dixon.

Scratching his clean chin Dixon replies "Yeah, feeling a lot clearer...and cleaner" he chuckles, snatching the bag from Jimmy.

"Jimmy, can you help, I think there's something wrong with Dixon," RJ says mockingly.

"Wow, what the hell?" Jimmy turns and sees the apartment. It's not miraculously become a super swanky looking hotel room or anything, but the change is astounding. The floor is clean, the kitchen doesn't have junk sitting all over it, there's a dryer with clean clothes draped over it, the dust collecting on the table and chairs is gone. It resembles a perfectly livable space.

"You cleaned!" Jimmy stands in awe of it all. Dixon chuckles again, thinking it a joking quip between friends. Taking the bottles of beer and the whisky out of the bag, he turns back to see Jimmy still gawking.

"Hey, Kersh!" Dixon frowns at the mannequin pose. Jimmy quickly turns around and manages to catch the beer Dixon tosses him.

"Are you feeling ok?" Dixon asks, with an inquisitive look. Jimmy shakes his head a little and blinks again.

"Yeah, uh, I'm just, this is weird to see again. Kind of makes me wonder if you really are doing better or if you've gone even deeper down the whole" *There's* the Jimmy that Dixon remembers. He gives him a pat on the shoulder as he passes and takes a seat. Jimmy looks at him until Dixon gestures to the other seat with his eyes, he takes a seat.

"So today was crazy…" Dixon says taking a swig of the beer he'd popped open. Jimmy nods in quiet response.

"Jimmy, make sure Dixon doesn't switch me off or mute me again, will you?" RJ asks. Jimmy smiles looking at Dixon's arm.

"I'd have you on mute constantly," says Jimmy.

"Scratching you off the Christmas card list," says RJ.

"I didn't know if I was going to get fucked up if I ever met that slimy nut pirate" Jimmy can't help but laugh at Dixon's forever colourful language. "I think I needed it" he pauses, looking off into the distance.

"I don't know if I could have killed him. I don't really remember actually much of it now, I only see his face all mashed up!" Dixon scowls, the memory of the blood, shattered teeth and clearly broken bones disgust him. The graphic devastation now a vile reminder of his closure.

"He's in hospital, doctors say they're going to need to build him a new nose and jaw," Jimmy says plainly, thinking in his head how much he wishes he could have inflicted the pain instead. He'd have been able to have the joy of delivering that justice, he'd also have kept Dixon from what appears to be a very challenging experience. He's already been through enough Jimmy thinks, although this is the best he's looked in years.

"Hey, uh, you didn't happen to notice what was written on those papers he had?" Dixon seems to flicker back into his body and resume being a normal human.

"Oh yeah, I wonder where he got them from. Maybe some weird collector's thing?" Jimmy swigs his beer pinching his brow.

"A douche nozzle like that? Yeah, I'm sure he collects old papers, Jimmy." RJ sharply interjects.

"They were legal documents for Fenghuang and Halo" Dixon points out, leaning his arm in his knees.

"Legal documents? Like a merger?" Jimmy pinches his brow further, Dixon nods. "Why use paper? They could just as easily put that shit online."

"Didn't think of it much at the time, but I can't get it out of my head now. There was mention of a merger between the two of them and a reconstruction of the GID tree" Dixon purses his lips trying to read Jimmy's reaction. "Presumably they want to keep it under wraps, off the grid, offline."

"Who reads books or magazines these days? It'd be easy to hide that kind of thing", RJ says plainly.

"Feng and Halo merger? Shit! That'd take the world to its knees. There wouldn't be anyone to compete with that." Jimmy lifts his gaze from the floor as he considers the information. Dixon's eyes stare back. Both men thinking how much this feels like their old work discussions, back in the day as rookies. Talking at great length about the conspiracies they'd "uncovered", new evidence, like they were both already detectives.

"What was the reconstruction? Are they planning on separating out the top tiers further? Let those shit biscuits at the top take even more power from everyone?" Jimmy leans back in his seat, glugging down more beer.

Dixon shakes his head, "No, they were *simplifying it* in their words." Jimmy tilts his head quizzically. "Exactly. Sounds iffy, doesn't it? They are wanting to bring the GIDs into just three official categories."

"We have five right now, right? I get confused at how those upper tier pricks class it!" Jimmy says.

"Yes, low, mid, high, executive, council. That's us right now, they want to make it low, high, council!" says RJ, Jimmy's eyes move to the side trying to figure things out.

"Ok, that does sound simpler" He bites his lip, trying to figure out what he's missing.

"It is, but this is Fenghuang, there's always a catch! The low and mid-levels get combined into one new low GID class. High's and executives become one new High-level GID and I'm guessing the council stays the cock shiners at the very top." As Dixon talks, Jimmy's gaze returns to the carpet.

"Fuck! Those bastards are going to make us all slaves!" Spit flails from Jimmy's lips. He drinks his beer, finishing it and slams it on the table. Dixon rises from his chair and walks to the refrigerator.

"Yup! They are going to take more power from people, you said it." Opening the refrigerator, Dixon grabs another beer and tosses it to Jimmy, he pops the lid off and looks into space again.

"Fuck!" Jimmy shouts after several quiet seconds. Standing from the seat, the two of them lean on the kitchen counter.

"We have to do something!" Jimmy shrugs looking at Dixon for an answer.

"Yup! We will." He takes a swig from his beer with a smile on his face.

"Well don't keep me in suspense, partner" Jimmy beckons.

"Partner?" Dixon and RJ say in unison. Jimmy doesn't reply but gestures both hands in the air for him to answer his curiosity. Dixon snickers, resting his beer on the table as his friend leans on his elbows.

"What do you say we give Chester another visit?" Dixon chugs the last of his beer down. Jimmy in a breath of growing excitement leans back. His signature cheeky smile crawling over his face again.

Chapter 7

Jimmy is overjoyed at the condition his best friend is in. He seems like he's back to his old self. The news of a secret deal reigniting the fire that made him want to be a detective in the first place. He could work with his old buddy again, not in an official capacity. There is no way that LAF would employ him again after his service. If they looked over any tracking camera videos of him over the past years they'd probably want to lock him up rather than reinstate him.

The captain hadn't seemed too bothered with the wreckage that had been made of Chester's face though. A real hard ass, with a boner for beating someone into their place, he laughed a belly laugh when he got the news, and told Jimmy he wished he'd seen it. He had no idea it was Dixon who had dished out the pummelling, and he didn't need to know if they two of them went on their own investigation. Hell, nobody really cared what or where Jimmy was. He was a mid-level detective, as far as all the other high-level detectives cared he was still just a regular cop. If he didn't pick up on the minion work, they'd just push it down the line to some dumbfounded officer.

"Hey, just thinking before we go see Chester, we should probably wait a few days. Let him get out of the hospital and think he's resting easy. We won't be able to give him an intense questioning in the hospital anyway, too many eyes" says Jimmy.

"He's right, Dixon, Fenghuang will probably have a warning to keep an eye out for you both," RJ says.

Dixon laughs "Intense questioning? That what you guys call your interrogation techniques now? You're right, we'll wait for him to get out of the hospital. In the meantime, we could go to the other guys"

"The other guys?" asks Jimmy.

"Halo. I'm sure we can find someone in the know or someone who knows someone in the know, you know?" says Dixon.

"I know," RJ says. Dixon smirks at his arm.

Jimmy grits his teeth "Isn't Sadie in close with Halo now?" his question is met with silence. Several seconds pass before Jimmy realises he hadn't heard the information from Dixon.

"Um..." RJ's digital voice lingers.

"Oh, yeah, uh, sorry buddy. She's in Denver working at Halo now. Some receptionist kind of job" Jimmy says as he realises that Dixon had been staring at a drawer in the kitchen. He walks to the drawer and slowly opens it, a mixture of random garbage tries to burst out. Dixon pulls a picture frame out of the drawer, a bright image sits in the frame. Dixon and Sadie in a warm embrace, Sadie kissing Dixon's cheek. Jimmy leans closer and asks "When was the last time you saw her?"

"Four years ago, she was in a bar I stumbled into. I barely recognized her. She was there with friends..." Dixon's eyes still fixed on the picture. "She was laughing and having a good time and her friends noticed me, I don't think they know me, I've never met them before. They kept pointing and laughing at me, probably because I was a wreck." Dixon swallows trying to contain his emotion. Jimmy looks on, curious to see if his best friend is going to open up more.

"They kept laughing, and I shouted at one of them when I finally recognized her. She was the only one that wasn't laughing at me. She still drowns out all the noise when I see her." Dixon stifles a tear, managing to hold his emotions in check only just. "Anyway, she came over and helped me up. Dusted me down. Told me I should really go home, and stopped the bartender from throwing me out. I think she called me a ride home, I can't remember. I just stared at her"

"I miss her," RJ says, a faint glitch in her voice.

"Maybe we shouldn't go and see her. I don't want you breaking down again." Jimmy takes the picture from Dixon and stands it on the counter, closing the drawer and gripping Dixon's shoulders. Dixon frowns a little. Jimmy's hands look tiny around his broad physique.

"No, we're going!" Dixon shrugs Jimmy's grip off and walks to the cupboard next to the front door. Opening it, he pats some dust off of a jacket on the hook. He takes the jacket and rolls his arms smoothly into the sleeves, it still fits well after all these years. Jimmy smiles and shakes his head, as Dixon opens the door and gives a smug nod.

"Ooh, he puts on a jacket, ooh!"

Chapter 8

Pulling up to the headquarters of Halo, Dixon and Jimmy are quickly picked up by the security system. Two guards approach, both wearing smart black suits gripping to the muscles held within them. Black helmets encapsulate their heads, presumably to both remove any sense of individuality and provide them with the heads up display to identify almost anyone. Both guards also wear Echo Armour' bodysuits, designed to hide the sounds of whoever is wearing it. Strange that these guards would need to be quiet, probably a statement of quality over practicality. Halo standard troop armour provides as much defence as anyone could ask for in Denver since it became filled with danger. They prided themselves on kitting out their own with the best kit.

Denver being one of the favourite places for people to swarm to, as the tides began to rise, unwanted types came along with it. The digital libraries filled with historical documents of the debates over climate change, and the scientific world displaying all the evidence they could to back it up. The world knew this was going to happen, and yet the world leaders scoffed at it. Their own arrogance drawing their focus to gaining more power, and securing their next term in office, idiots!

Of course, the sea levels were predicted to rise a <u>small</u> amount, and they did, to begin with. After twenty years passed, North America lost fifteen percent of its land mass; the scientists were taken more seriously. Those that were left that is. Many people died as their homes were swallowed up by the oceans. It was predicted that the most deaths occurred during panicked evacuations of coastal cities.

Fortunately for the world, the geniuses working at Leistung brought forward an age of clean energy. Clean energy that they provided to the world, at a price. Deals with other firms took place, and Leistung put up footholds across the globe, each one guarded by dedicated Leistung mercs. Every single one also surrounded by the respective power of that regions military. With the boom in energy, Fenghuang was able to focus their scientific divisions to cleaning the atmosphere, healing the earth, you might say. The only selfless thing they have ever done; Fenghuang still talks of it to this day. Sure, they technically saved the planet, but why would you want to continue expanding your empire if the planet was a desolate husk.

"Good day, gentlemen. Do you have an appointment?" the first faceless goon asked. Jimmy looks down, flashing his holo-badge.

"No appointment, guys. We're needing to speak with Sadie Knight" Jimmy looks at both guards, the small lights that trace patterns around their skulls circulating around a Halo logo on each of their temples. The second guard lowers the energy rifle he holds. Dixon turns his head to look at Jimmy, confused.

"She changed her last na-"

The guard cuts him off "No appointment, no entry I'm afraid". Dixon turns to face the guards, annoyed that he cut him off.

"Many people come here with appointments for receptionists?" His tone ringing hard, the guards both readjusting their rifles.

"Leave the premises immediately", the order clear.

"Or what?" RJ exclaims. Both guards look down to Dixon's arm, one tilts his head slightly.

"Excuse me, do we have a misunderstanding here?" Jimmy steps forward. "Did you not notice?" he flashes his badge again.

"I know you Halo boys might be kitted out in the flashiest shit since holographic pornography, but don't think that gives you the right to interfere with a LAF investigation!" Jimmy stops his face inches from the first guard's helmet.

"Run my face again - Detective Jimmy Kershon - here to meet with Sadie Knight." Dixon watches, impressed with how Jimmy handles himself. The lights on both guards helmet zip around quickly and blink green. Both drop the rifles and turn to their sides, allowing Jimmy and Dixon to pass.

"Apologies, sir. We've informed Sadie Knight of your arrival. Please enjoy your visit to Halo HQ!"

Jimmy leads the way, as Dixon sniggers while walking past.

"Yeah, that's right, out of the way, peons!" RJ says sharply but quietly.

"How many times a day do you do that trick?" Dixon asks, catching up.

"First time I've done that in a while. Those security guards are mid-level, if the security system didn't approve us through, then scaring them with suspensions would have" Jimmy smirks back.

Two more guards stand at the door entrance as they approach. Clear glass slides apart in what seems like ten different directions to open the door. Stepping inside, it almost feels like a new world in itself. White walls hold blue highlight strips which seem to follow behind every person walking around. Each person almost robotic in their path. A spherical ball, held on a long arm, extends out of what Dixon thought was an artistic sculpture.

The orb blips into life, three blue lights forming a line in its centre. "Good day, Detective Kershon, Dixon Callaway. Your appointment with Sadie Knight is set to take place on the seventy-fourth flour in room Seven, Four, Q, B" says a polite female English voice. Dixon quirks his head back. Jimmy nudges him to remain calm.

"Please feel free to use our grav-lifts while in the building" The three lines morphing into an arrow, point to the series of metal doors surrounding two giant pillars that seem to stretch to the roof of the building.

"Thanks," Jimmy says as he walks off, Dixon stuttering before joining him.

"I don't like her," RJ says.

"Me neither" Dixon whispers down to RJ.

"Grav-lifts? These guys are fucking with gravity now?" Dixon slaps Jimmy on the shoulder.

"It's not gravity in that sense. Closer to some magnetism or energy based thing. Sorry, I'm no physics geek. The dweebs at Leistung have been wanting to get their hands on it for years now" Jimmy laughs "think they are tired of walking upstairs".

"Thought they had regular hydraulic lifts?" asks Dixon.

"They do, they also provide the power to make these grav-lifts work. Halo isn't giving up the plans for them though." They approach one of the doors, three lights slide on at the top of the door and quickly scan their faces. The doors part and the same voice from the orb speaks again.

"Please enter" Once they've stepped inside the doors close. "Ascending" The voice states.

"Ascending? Jesus, no wonder these pompous fucks think so highly of themselves" RJ remarks. Dixon taps his arm, disciplining RJ for swearing.

"You don't feel like you're ascending to the heavens," Jimmy says, winking.

The ride up takes seconds. As the doors open, the voice pleasantly states "Arrived at destination". The two-step out, and a highlight in the wall glows a greener tone than the blue they'd seen when they entered. Jimmy approaches it, and the green blip slowly begins to move off down the corridor to the left.

"Guess we have a guide," Jimmy says, shrugging to Dixon.

"Pompous fucks!" Dixon grumbles, following Jimmy. Several people pass by them in the opposite direction as they are lead around the maze of corridors. The building itself is fully automated and controlled by artificial intelligence. They pass by a kitchen area where machines take food orders and dispense the requests into trays and bowls. Various people sit around making small talk. All of them wearing similar white business outfits with blue stripes on the hems.

Finally, the green light stops and blinks three times. The door opposite a sheet of white with a blue light displayed on it.

As the green light begins to fade RJ says. "I don't like that either"

"Seven Four Q B, uh thanks, Greeny" Jimmy say to the blip as it fades off.

"Don't name the fucking thing" Dixon says as they enter the room.

"Dixon!" A female voice says sharply.

Dixon ,whipping his eyes to the origin, freezes.

"Hello Sadie," Jimmy says.

Chapter 9

"How've you been?" Sadie asks with a warm smile.

"Great thanks" Jimmy replies, popping his collar in a joking fashion "Detective now!"

"That's great, Jimmy" Sadie turns her head to Dixon, looking him up and down as he stands still, gawking.

"Are you going to sit down, Dixon?" She asks, lowering her head.

"Hi Sadie, I've missed you so much," says RJ. Sadie frowns a little, looking at Dixon's arm.

"You still have her plugged in there?" Sadie asks, quizzical at first, her expression softens as she looks into Dixon's eyes.

He shakes his head quickly, his jaw quivering as he slides into his chair. Sadie had always said that he'd grown too attached to RJ. An appliance he'd affectionately named after his daughters as some sort of coping mechanism. He should have had the device restored to default settings, and the AI replaced. She didn't have the heart to really tell him to get rid of RJ though. It was hard enough to have to let go of their children, let alone watch someone else struggle with it. Jimmy and Dixon sit on either side of Sadie as she slips into the chair at the head of the long conference table.

"Sorry, I uh, you changed your name" Dixon's eyes looking kindly at his ex-wife.

"Well, we're no longer married" Sadie's tone blunt and to the point. She turns back to Jimmy, smiling slightly.

"They didn't say it was you who was needing to see me. Don't think I'd have been as nervous if I knew." Dixon's eyes take in her image again like it was the first time seeing her. Her suit jacket and skirt looking more expensive than Dixon's entire collection of clothing, not surprisingly. Her hair well styled, coloured silver and draped to one side. A plainer colour of lipstick painted onto her lips with a blue edge to them. Her eyes a bluer shade than Dixon had remembered. Jimmy kicks him under the table as he notices him ogling.

"We tend not to operate with names when we need to question someone." says Jimmy.

"Am I in trouble?" Sadie's eyes flicking back and forth from Jimmy to Dixon.

"No, no. We just came into some information and wondered if you'd be able to help us." Jimmy pulls his sleeve up and presses the display in his forearm. A holographic bust of Chester Lopez displays. "Do you recognize this man?"

"What the fuck is going on?" Sadie's face contorting, warping to disgust and then to fury. Dixon's face also pinches a little at the sight. "Why are you showing me *his* face?"

"There was a disturbance in his apartment, we did a routine check in to make sure all was well." Jimmy swipes at the bust and it shrinks back into his display.

"We? You're not back on the force are you, Dixon?" She gasps.

"This guy? God no!" RJ says.

"No, they wouldn't let me even if I wanted to be. Jimmy invited me along to meet that little prick" he replies.

"Oh my god, you killed him didn't you" Sadie's face trembles.

"He's alive" Jimmy interjects.

"Alive? What the hell did you do to the guy?" asks Sadie. Leaning on the table, her chest pounding.

Dixon leans onto the table, looking deep into his ex-wife's eyes. "I beat that fuck who took our girls. I beat him within an inch of his life. He didn't even recognize me. Now nobody will recognize who he is!" Dixon's muscles tighten as he talks. Sadie looks down and leans back into the chair. Her breathing still heavy, she puts a hand on her chest trying to calm down. Her mind trying to figure out how to respond, how to feel.

"I hate that guy. I really hate that guy, Dixon. He's the man who is responsible for the worst part of my life." She looks up at Dixon, tears slowly emerging.

"You look good, I haven't seen you look that good in a long time. Please don't tell me this is some story of vengeance you're on. You're done with him, right?" A tear runs down her cheek, the blue eyeshadow lightly staining her skin. Dixon reaches over and lightly takes her hand.

"I'm done with him, Sadie. I blacked out when it happened. When I got home all I could think of was our girls. I still miss them." Dixon says. Jimmy remains as quiet as possible, seeing more emotion being held back in Dixon than he's seen in quite some time.

Sadie removes her hand and rests them in her lap. Another tear runs down her face. "So, uh, what was this all about, huh? Just wanted to come here and tell me you beat the hell out of the guy who killed our daughters?" She wipes her eyes. Jimmy leans forward, pulling out a handkerchief and offering it to Sadie. She curls her lips and accepts.

"While we were in Chester's apartment we came across a document, or Dixon did at least. Legal documents, printed on real paper, mentioning a merger and a reconstruction of sorts." Jimmy looks to Dixon, catching his eye, the former LAF cop regains some composure.

"So what? Mergers happen all the time. Are they reconstructing some building? Would make sense if there is a merger." Sadie sniffs away more tears and calms herself.

"Worse, a lot worse" chimes RJ.

"The merger is of Halo and Fenghuang. I've heard of mergers before, countless times, but never two heavy hitters like this." Sadie looks at Dixon in shock as he talks. "They aren't planning on reconstructing a building. They want to reconstruct the GIDs."

"Fenghuang? They want to merge with us? I haven't seen anything like that come through here" Sadie's brow narrows.

"Big surprise, huh?" says RJ, Dixon shrugs a little jokingly.

"That's why we believe it was printed on actual paper. Keep it from eyes who might oppose it. Would you see those kind of documents anyway?" Jimmy asks.

"I'm a receptionist for Leanne Watkins, she's part of Tom's legal team. If there was any document like that, it would have to have gone through her, so I'd have organised it for her." Sadie flutters her eyelids as she returns matter at hand.

"Tom?" Dixon asks.

"Tom Sutcliffe, big cheese of Halo," says RJ not liking the sound of the news.

"Tom wouldn't want to merge with Fenghuang, anyway. I've met him, he's a good person. I'm pretty sure he hates them." Sadie looks around as she contemplates possibilities. "Wait, reconstruct the GIDs?"

Dixon's grits his teeth, "Yes, they want all low and mid-levels to be combined. The highs and executives become one new high level and only the council level are left at the very top. Bet Fenghuang and Halo would be excited to have so much cheap labour available to them."

Sadie's eyes widen, her eyes still darting around. "No. No, that can't be. The number of resources they would be able to automate with that level of labour. They'd take over the world. They'd have an army four times the size and four times as powerful." She looks at Dixon.

"All those Fenghuang numbers armed to the teeth with the latest Halo tech. Who could stop them?" Dixon raises his eyebrows.

"We can," Jimmy says confidently. Both Dixon and Sadie guffaw at the idea.

"A cop, an ex-cop and a receptionist take down two of the biggest corporations in the world. Real fucking *movie like,* Kersh" Dixon shakes his head.

"Don't forget me!" RJ says, Dixon frowns.

"How would we do that, Jimmy?" Sadie looks at him sarcastically.

"We can put pressure on Chester. Before we were just inquiring into a domestic disturbance. Imagine how much information we can get out of him if we ask him about the merger." Jimmy smiles, his cheeky grin making Dixon smile a little also.

"Well, he'll recognize me this time I'm sure, but how does that help us stop this from going ahead?" Dixon asks, smiling, thinking he's caught his friend. His investigation skills still catching up to his friends. Jimmy gestures with open hands.

"He's going to be scared shitless. You'll terrify him enough, and if that doesn't then I'm sure he'll get edgy when LAF want to enquire why Halo and Fenghuang are playing their cards so close to their chest. While we're doing that - you can go to work." Jimmy points to Sadie.

"Me?" asks Sadie.

"Her?" asks Dixon.

"Her?" asks RJ.

"Her. I'm sure you've got some level of access to stuff around here. Start digging around. Look for anything that would point to, or would accompany this merger. Movement of assets, changing of departments. If there's anything on the reconstruction, then it'll damn sure be adjustments in staff placement, and who'll be taking orders from who." Jimmy stands from his chair and walks around as he explains. The two of them eagerly looking at him as the plan unfolds.

"I'll do my best, some of the stuff may be restricted" Sadie adds.

"The most incriminating stuff would be. The sort of things we're looking for won't be I'm betting. They'll want everything to be ready to go through pretty fast once the deal goes ahead.

We're not building a legal case. We're gathering ammunition"
Jimmy turns to face the two, eyebrows raised waiting for their
reaction.

"Ammunition, to take them down? But this isn't a legal case?"
Sadie says, still confused.

"Ammunition for who?" Dixon's gears start to pick up pace as
he begins to figure it out.

"Leistung!" Jimmy smiles.

Chapter 10

"Leistung?" Sadie, RJ and Dixon ask.

"Yup. Once we get all we can from Chester, and Sadie picks up all she can from the Halo servers, we can go to Leistung. They'll damn sure be interested" says Jimmy.

"Are you trying to recruit them?" Dixon stands from his chair.

"Gentlemen!" A voice burst into the room. The three all turn as a tall woman enters. Her stick like figure making her seem like some giant elf-like creature. Long blonde hair curled down her back, a narrow slit revealing her face. From what can be made out, she is not a woman of tremendous beauty, though her presence would state that she is a person to be heard and respected.

"And you are?" Dixon enquires.

"I'm so sorry, Miss Watkins" Sadie quickly stands from the chair and drops her head in a submissive pose.

"Sadie, what are these gentlemen doing here?" Watkins asks, as she tilts her head upward, her hair parting further to reveal her aged face, a small straight scar running across the right side of her face from her eye to her ear. She looks down at Dixon and across to Jimmy, her disapproval the only thing cutting the tension.

"This is Detective Kershon," Sadie says as she gestures at Jimmy, head still down. "And this is Dixon Callaway, my uh, ex-husband." She looks up, slightly nervous, trying to judge her bosses reaction. Miss Watkins clasps her hands as her head swivels to look at Jimmy. Her right iris swirling into blue light, the light shooting down her scar behind her hair. Raising her eyebrow, she looks Jimmy up and down a little, before turning to Dixon and doing the same. The blue light zipping back up the scar to her eye and spins back into her iris before fading.

"And I'm RJ" Dixon tries to cover his arm as she calls out. Watkins looks at his arm and back to his eyes, smiling cynically.

"What is the reason for this line of questioning, detective? I was not informed of this interruption to my employee's work schedule." She steps towards Jimmy, seeming to almost float. Both Jimmy and Dixon try to figure out if she is even human. An angel perhaps? Too old looking. A demon? Not evil looking enough. A robot seems just as viable an option as the others.

A little intimidated, being almost a foot shorter than Dixon and now presumably a foot and half shorter than this woman Jimmy responds. "We, uh, we're just here to see Sadie, to inform her of some news regarding the criminal who crashed into her and Dixon when they were uh…" he coughs uneasily.

"Married? Yes, I've seen the record of that accident" Presumably she'd gathered the information when Sadie had applied for the job. She may easily have also gathered the information from the scan she carried out on Jimmy and Dixon. Watkins takes a long breath in her beak like nose "good news?" A small smile creeps along her cracked face.

"Good news, indeed" Dixon slips his hands in his pockets, he is slightly intimidated by her. Watching her float around the room with a clear disdain for the "lowers" in the room, he remembers his own disgust for those of a privileged life.

"Do tell?" Watkins turns, bringing her fingertips together, her excitement matched with an inhuman callousness. Dixon looks across the room to Sadie. She's managed to raise her head and watch everything before her. He musters a half smile at the woman who once loved him. He can see the anxious fear she has of this woman.

"No, this was a personal matter" he turns back to face the thin old tree. "You understand", he manages to manifest a smile on his face. So fake and rare a smile that Jimmy is repulsed but it.

"Yeah, you understand" RJ backs him up.

"Hmm, of course. Sadie? Please return to your duties" Watkins says, without breaking eye contact with Dixon. Sadie nods and makes for the door.

"Right away, Miss Watkins" as she passes and leaves the room, looking back at Jimmy and Dixon. Her eyes wide and anxious, but pouring frustration at the two of them.

"Well" Jimmy sighs comically, "we'd best be off". He looks at Dixon, hinting for their departure.

"Gentlemen" they both halt their escape. Watkins straightens her back and looks to the back of the room. "If you need to speak to Miss Knight again please contact me. I like to be aware of any possible hindrance in my efficiency, or my staff directly beneath me."

"Sure thing" Jimmy mumbles, through gritted teeth "ma'am". His eyes flashing to Dixon, who stares back confused. Clearly, he is no longer daunted by her.

"Right, so can you show us out of this fucking ant farm?" Dixon pipes up. His words cutting through Watkins demeanour. She blinks and looks to him slowly, smiling as she does.

"The building shall return you to the lobby" She gestures her hand at the wall. The green blip returns on the wall. "I must leave you. Please have a good day, gentlemen" Her tone almost stabbing. She walks down the corridor, and disappears off into the white and blue on another. Jimmy turns back, adjusts his collar again, and lets out a large breath.

"Fuck, she was like some kind of cyber witch or something, huh?" Jimmy says, still a little creeped out.

"Yeah, or a rotting statue" Dixon still looks off in the direction she left with a lip turned. Jimmy slaps his arm and nods his head in the direction the blip is motioning.

"At least we got Greeny back!" Jimmy chuckles, and pats the wall where the green blip emanates. Dixon shakes his head, sighing heavily.

"I still don't like it," says RJ.

"This kind of shit explains why you're still single" Dixon quips.

As they are lead out of the building, Dixon notices that the few people they do pass almost seem to be in a trance-like state. Jimmy eyes them also, and leans in to whisper.

"I've heard they use conditioning and drug psychosis on some of their staff, keep them working for a long as they can" One of the ghost-like figures slides past the two of them without any emotion on his face.

"I thought they just used coffee for that kind of shit, you think they're doing that to Sadie?" Dixon leans across the path of another woman who is approaching. Her gaze doesn't falter, her face doesn't express anything.

"She seemed actually human in comparison to these zombies." They enter the lift again and descend to the ground floor, both looking around feeling watched. Jimmy continues as they exit the lift. "If anything, I guess she's just a little creeped out by her boss and doesn't want to get herself in the shit, huh?"

Dixon grunts in response. As they walk out the door, the orb statue morphs into life again, blinking on and calling out "Goodbye, gentlemen. We hope you had a good experience at Halo and have a peaceful day." They shrug off the feeling of unease as they jump into Jimmy's car and speed off.

"Where to now then? Chester?" Dixon's eyes light up as he asks.

"Seems reasonable. First let's swing by the precinct. I want to see if there's any other information came in about our little friend. I have a sneaking suspicion he'll have made some move since we last saw him" Jimmy manoeuvres around traffic quickly. There are so little actual cars around this region that it's easy for him to navigate around the automated transport vehicles working for Halo.

Chapter 11

The LAF precinct looks as impressive as one could expect from any building in the area. Downtown Denver is an unfriendly looking place. Everyone strolling the streets has an abundance of clothes to cover up their face. The clothes may be bright and showing off big brand name logos, but you'd be hard-pressed to figure out if it was a man or woman hiding beneath the outfits. Even judging a person's size and physique is difficult when an old punk style leather jacket with spikes, covers a trench coat painted with digi-tribal patterns along the length. A green skull face across a scarf that covers the mouth, and a bandana with the eyes cut out, covering the top half of the head. This particular figure trying to flirt with Jimmy as they park up in the car park. Most of the spaces are assigned to LAF officers, but the public doesn't care anymore; they park where they want and some homeless people even set up camp in spots.

"Hey little guy, looking for something special?" The figure yammers at Jimmy, the eyes peeking out from behind the black bandana showing the only sense of humanity under the garb. Jimmy doesn't care for this spin on humanity either.

"Special?" He steps to the figure. "What special thing you going to give to an LAF Detective?" He flashes his holo-badge and waits for a reply. The figure looks him up and down, followed by Dixon and chuckles softly.

"You LAF boys. You work too hard. You guys need to relax a little", the eyes smile, staring back.

"Is this, THING, a prostitute?" Dixon is almost amused by the creature soliciting them. The figure pulls back, clearly offended by the remark. Grabbing the jacket and flinging it open the figure reveals itself. A middle-aged man, slightly malnourished, his bones and muscle hauntingly visible. Patches of his skin look blotchy and unhealthy. What little skin that doesn't look infected, is poking through metal parts, wires leap around his chest. Metal pistons churn in his stomach, he reaches up to his scarf and yanks it down. The entirety of his jaw has been reconstructed with large metal pieces. Seemingly put together from various pieces of rusting metal and assorted pieces, the cheek muscles are bonded to it. A horrific smile appears from the half human half machine creature.

"Something to take the edge off?" Jimmy eventually manages to notice the array of pockets littered around the inside of the jacket. Drugs, upon drugs, upon drugs. The selection is impressive and the attention to detail more so. Embossed sticky labels have been attached to each pocket with the names and prices of the drugs. The labels infused with neon to make them pop in the evening light. Jimmy scowls at the creature and grabs his shoulder, spinning him and shoving him down the road.

"Get out of here. If I see you when I'm on the way out I'm putting you in the hole!" Jimmy shouts, as the man shimmies off down the road. Turning to Dixon he shrugs, "Fuckin junkies, man. It'd be easier to lock them up if half the crooked cops upstairs didn't use them".

"His mods didn't look in good shape, how does he have that many anyway?" asks Dixon.

"Most of the junkies around here have similar kind of shit. Simulated livers, artificial lungs, fake bladders. They get hooked on the drugs and nearly kill themselves" Jimmy pushes the door of LAF open, Dixon nods as he listens. "They ruin their organs and shit, but still need to get their fix so they either sell enough drugs themselves to buy a mod, or let some wannabe botch modder try out a fix for them." Says Jimmy.

"Botch modders? I thought all modding was regulated." Dixon glowers.

"Doesn't matter how many mods he gets, he can't fix that kind of ugly" RJ quips. Dixon and Jimmy grin.

"It was regulated, and it still is to a degree but even the big wigs will occasionally go for something a little more risqué. For those junkies, it's like jumping the border to Mexico to get some shifty, cockeyed surgeon to stitch you up. The junkies are too tweaked out to notice that they're getting plugged into old car batteries, and having one hundred and fifty-year-old motherboard and tech shoved in them." Jimmy leads Dixon up to the third floor of the building. Keeping his head low, only a couple of heads turn to double take at him, nobody seems to be able to place him.

The walls bring back memories of a slightly similar time. Working with Jimmy had been, for the most part, a fond memory. The two of them picking up cases and challenging each other to make more elaborate and convoluted explanations for why murders took place. Chuckling occasionally, as they would build elaborate stories of families torn apart by debt and hidden affairs, "it's always the spouse" they'd laugh. When it came down to it though, Jimmy was always the one to step into question a suspect or victim. His *by the book* procedure was admirable. Dixon, on the other hand, saw the darker side in humanity. He had "street smarts" - is what most people would call it. He'd regularly find himself having to pick apart a situation by stomping into it. Jimmy would try to reason with words, while Dixon used his fists. This worked for the duo, their success rate was among the highest in their department. It's probably why Jimmy managed to get promoted to detective. Dixon suspected it was more so because Jimmy really was a stickler for detail. After they'd get back to the precinct and throw the perps into their cells, Jimmy would get to work on his report. Dixon, sharing the mindset of most of his fellow officers, the report didn't matter as much; As long as the bad guys were behind bars. Jimmy would regularly reel Dixon back in though, sit him down, and help him through the tedious pencil work.

The doors to the bull pit open and desks are manned by several attractive women. All with their hair tied back and sharp spectacles perched on their noses. Their clothing reminiscent of a forty's or fifty's era, although they each wear a wraparound LAF headset that's plugged into their glasses. The lenses seem to flicker and flash as data zooms across them. The receptionists for the detectives, carry out the task of sifting through the garbage cases that get escalated and circulated, to try and find their superior something juicy. Sitting on the front of each desk is a name, not the woman's but the detective she has been assigned to. Dixon looks around quickly taking in as many names as he can.

"Where's your receptionist?" Dixon asks.

"Oh they are only for the *real* detectives," Jimmy says using air quotes.

"Ah! How lucky they are. Did they feed you some bullshit for not getting one?" Dixon asks as Jimmy nods while opening his office door. His name printed on the stained window. Jimmy takes his coat off and tosses it at a coat hanger, it lands perfectly. Dixon looks around at the selection of boxes, each one holds a further plethora of smaller boxes. Inside, several data grids lie collecting dust. Scrawled over the boxes, an assortment of names glower towards Jimmy's desk. He slumps down into his chair, a mould bitten old thing. Stained material from the early twenty-one hundreds edging out from tears, and probably hosting some form of life.

"Busy then?" Dixon gestures at the boxes.

"Don't get me started on all this shit." Jimmy sits up, pointing in turn at a few boxes. "Lost dog, ex stole my keys, owes me money, killed my cousin" His face drops further and further with each mention.

"Killed my cousin?" Dixon's voice perks interest.

"Nah, it's bullshit. Asshole is ninety-six years old and calls up almost every month saying someone is gone. His cousin died of mod induced cancer some twenty years ago." Pressing a button on his desk, Jimmy looks to the drawer, it doesn't budge. He presses again, still nothing – again – still nothing. Jimmy shakes his head and grumbles, smashing the button with a fist. The drawer bleeps and slides open. Grabbing a bottle of whisky and two glasses he signals Dixon, he nods.

"Sounds like the guy needs a carer," RJ says, her voice soft.

"Not wrong, RJ, you're not wrong," Jimmy says pouring drinks. "He has a carer, the guy is too busy trying to sell drugs in the nursing home though. Everyone is a piece of shit these days".

"You really are getting the shit end of *dick stick* then, huh?" Dixon takes the half-full glass from Jimmy and clinks it, the two take a large gulp.

"Captain's a good guy, I guess. Doesn't ride my ass. He doesn't stop all the other pricks around here from doing what they can to make sure I know I'm not one of them." Jimmy looks into the bottom of his glass, sighing as his throat burns. "Guess I'm the lucky one for getting here". Jimmy ironically smiles before putting his glass down and tapping another button on his desk. A square in front of him tilts up and lights blink to life. Jimmy begins swiping and tapping at the holo-display. His wrist flickering to life also and syncing up the data from his last check-in.

"Well look at this!" Jimmy smiles while exhaling. He hints to Dixon, who gulps down the last of his whisky before leaning towards the desk. Jimmy swipes the image up from his display. The tilted display raises itself to become flat and protruding out of the desk. The holo-display adjusts and a cube morphs into view. A picture of the front of Chester's building can be seen.

"Looks like Mr Lopez has got him some boys to keep watch" Jimmy taps the cube, and each side of the cube displaying the picture plays the video. Chester walks out of the front of the building with two large figures, both wearing Phoenix helmets and long black trench coats. The collars of each flicking a line of red light along it every few seconds. A small bird displayed on the chest of each coat also. Dixon's scratches his forehead. Talons.

"Those guys look friendly" Dixon remarks as another two gentlemen walk out wearing similar garb. Chester points one in either direction before they walk out of view.

"He must be scared shitless if he's got Talons on lookout. They aren't cheap ones either. He's got some privileges if he's getting that tier of Talon." Jimmy smiles a little, but inside he's getting quite nervous. "I'm pretty sure those guys are mainly reserved for the top executives or council member protection."

"Why does that little shit stain need so much security?" Dixon stands, adjusting his jacket.

Jimmy looks up from the table, throwing back the last of his whisky. "Exactly"

"So what the hell are we going to do now? Looks like they are covering all entrances." Dixon reaches for the door.

Jimmy crumples his face while thinking. A lightbulb almost springing to life as his gears click to an answer. "When was the last time you saw, Gizzy?"

Chapter 12

"Gizzy is still alive?" Dixon asks, chasing Jimmy down the stairs of the precinct towards the basement level.

"We're still wondering if anything can kill him" Jimmy looks back over his shoulder. They pass the prisoner level with a large metal double door. Giant bars span the entire door, and are held in place by the identification lock. Voices can be heard moaning and shouting expletives. Descending further they reach the bottom floor. "Armoury" is written in block letters across the wall. Many large bars stretch from the roof to the floor. Lining the edge of the bars, floor, and ceiling, are laser wires. The faint buzz can be heard as the wires power the bars with enough energy to wipe out a blue whale, if there were any left in the world.

Jimmy tries to look around the bars and sees a large warehouse of toys. Tables full of clothes and priceless personal possessions, all jumbled up into boxes. The walls are lined with hooks holding every variation of weapon one could imagine; pistols, rifles, shotguns, grenade launchers, rocket launchers, energy weapons, mag weapons, rail guns - all with a tag hanging from them. An ID number, model and nickname given to them. On the next set of hooks down are several "homemade" weapons. Presumably lifted from an assortment of criminals; knives and makeshift guns hang with varying levels of rust.

"Hey, Giz?" Jimmy shouts, a small echo of a rumble can be heard at the back. A door leading off the warehouse opens, light pouring out of it followed by a frustrated voice.

"Huh?" The rasp of the voice easily recognizable.

"Who's Gizzy?" RJ whispers to Dixon, he ignores.

"Giz, it's me, Jimmy?" Jimmy continues to look, trying to see through the door.

"Jimmy? Who the fuck is Jimmy?" A cough follows, filled with phlegm and hate

Jimmy sighs "Detective Kershon!" There is a moment of silence before a bump and grumble ring through the warehouse. A whistling churns every few seconds as a body emerges through the door, sitting in a wheelchair, an old wheelchair from before Jimmy or Dixon's grandfather's days. The frame hooked up with some more modern day wires and stabilizers to give it more reliable control and power. Perched on it a man, looking as old as time, stares through half closed eyes. His face hanging on only by the resentment emanating from his bittered soul. The wheelchair rolls up to the small window between four of the bars. His yellow eyes fixate on Jimmy as the chair begins to rise, extending the man into a standing position. Dixon is sure he hears a couple of cracks as the ancient body reaches its peak.

"That's better. I told you kid, always with the detective!" Gizzy's lips spread to reveal a yellow toothed smile. "Otherwise they'll give you some shitty nickname like Gizmo. Then they'll lock you down here and forget about you"

"Yeah, I know Gizzy. Hey, I've got someone here you might have forgotten." Jimmy steps aside, as Dixon slowly moves forward. Gizzy's eyes focus together at the figure.

"Giz, I thought you were dead, old man" Dixon's voice widening Gizmo's eyes.

"This is Gizzy?" RJ whispers again, unimpressed.

"Dixon fucking Callaway" his festering smile crawls across his face again. "I thought you were busy drinking your ass into a stupor. You pulled that mountain of shit you call a body out of the bottom of the bottle, huh? And as for you - miss cheeky AI. I've been around since before your ones and zeros bumped uglies to make you."

"I like him," RJ says, with a hint of laughter.

"Glad you remember me" Dixon unable to hide the warmth he feels. He always enjoyed the mutual ripping of each other with Gizmo. "That a new chair?"

"Don't get funny with me you little shit. I may be old but I'll still kick your ass" The fire still in his eyes, Dixon can't help but admire Gizmo's intensity. "Had an upgrade to this pussy wagon. If you could call it that"

"Definitely like him" RJ confirms.

"Oh yeah?" Dixon tilts his head, looking down on him jokingly.

"It whacked out on me one day, so they plugged me directly into the chair" Gizmo points a thumb to the back of his neck. Dixon notices the circuitry and wiring tying him to the chair via his spine.

"At least I can control it on my own now, no joystick or nothing. 'Bout as close to walking as I'll ever get." With that Gizmo hunches down and up a couple of times as he spins in a circle, giggling. "Now, are you two just here to jack me off, or do you want something?"

"Be the most action Jimmy's seen in years" remarks RJ. Gizmo laughs and points to Dixon's arm while looking at Jimmy.

"I like her" he states.

Jimmy smirks "We need your help, old timer. Planning on going to see a certain Fenghuang employee. He's got some pretty heavy duty security lingering around, figure you can hook us up?" Gizmo balls up his lips - considering the problem. His eyes look up suddenly as he swipes his finger on the touchpad of his wheelchair. Four of the bars beside the window suddenly shoot down allowing Dixon and Jimmy to enter.

As they pass through, the bars dart back into place with a weighty clunk. The buzz from the laser wire fizzing a little as they extend the circuit again. Gizmo returns to a seated position and spins around, leading the two of them down an aisle between tables of personal belongings.

"Talons?" He asks not looking back.

"Yup," Dixon picks at some strange belongings he sees amongst the selection. Small keychains, toothbrushes, children's toys, and even a backpack filled to the brim with screwdrivers and wrenches.

A grunt bellows from Gizmo as he turns a corner heading towards the weaponry. "Evil people those Feng's. Never liked them. One of this filthy shits put me in this chair" He rolls past some weapons to a chest sitting under one of the tables.

"What's in this?" Jimmy asks, while investigating the box. Gizmo stares back with a cheeky grin and a raised eyebrow. He turns to Dixon and nods his head,

"You'll never get it open, kid. You're too dumb." Dixon laughs at the insult, RJ displays a face crying with laughter on his arm. "Go on Dixon, give it a try," Gizmo points to the chest. Dixon shrugs and gives it a wallop with his boot. It reels back on its hinges and springs to life. Metal cogs turn and light up, a small display window tilts out of the top. The three of them look at it as if it had woken up and cried for help. "Give it another" Gizmo says leaning into Dixon. He obliges and wallops the box again. This time the box simply rocks back, and slams down. Gizmo nods at it, then to Jimmy and Dixon.

"Hey. That isn't going to work. I've seen one of these before. This is an old Valkyrie box." Jimmy kneels down at the display, looking over the menu which asks for identification.

"No shit, Sherlock. Where'd you get that from?" Gizmo barks again as he points at the large logo sprayed across the front. A winged woman, wearing a pointed helmet, looks to the sky as a large golden V stands in front of her. Jimmy looks up with a sarcastic smile.

"These guys got swallowed up by Halo, and I think most of their guys work R and D now." Jimmy's hands hover over the display. He brings his forearm display to life, and begins to play with it as Gizmo turns to Dixon.

"It came in about four years ago. Some Halo shipment coming in from the east coast that got hit big time by some modder gang. Halo was more interested in getting the new tech back than this old piece of junk." He rolls off from the box, motioning Dixon to join him. "It's been collecting dust, we couldn't get authorisation to open it, and after a while, nobody could be bothered to figure out the lock." As he reaches for one of the mag rifles perched on hooks, he hears an unfamiliar voice.

"Identification Accepted" a plain female voice states. He turns around to see the box top split in two and curl out to reveal the contents. Jimmy looks over, a picture of smugness. He stands and holds his hands out.

"No way," says RJ.

"Too dumb, huh?" He raises his shoulders and looks back to the contents of the box, squinting as he tries to figure out what it is. He reaches in and pulls out several large bodysuits. The large V of the Valkyrie logo displayed on the front. The woman ascending to the heavens stencilled on the back. "You know what these are?" Jimmy asks the other two, as his face begins to light up. They return to him and look blank faced, awaiting the answer.

"They're Valkyrie power armour suits." He says, gaping at the craftsmanship. "I didn't think these still existed. Valkyrie wore these when they were fighting off Zero Round in Alberta, Canada. Took Halo six months to take them down because these babies kept Valkyrie going." He reaches into the box and pulls out another suit. Checking the size he throws it to Dixon.

Dixon catches it and inspects it. "So what makes these things so special?"

"Valk-suits absorb almost any energy weapon. They'll hold back a knife with ease, and keep whoever wears it from going up in flames." Jimmy's eyes continue to explore the suit, finding the hidden zip in the back. Dixon squints as he tries to look for the zip on his.

"So why did they get rid of these things then? And why didn't we get these when LAF started contracting out for those Halo dicks."

Gizmo looks back and forth at the suits. "Too bulky, they were a little too heavy for their liking. Nowhere near sleek enough for them, and once Halo took over, they created a new upgraded version. One with biostatistics tracking." He wheels forward, taking a hold of the arm of Jimmy's suit. "They wanted to track their boys, and liked the thought of using the suits rather than LAF's arm links." He nods at the display on Jimmy's arm.

"Think anyone would notice if we took them?" Jimmy asks anxiously.

"Kid, nobody even knows they're here" Jimmy backpedals and continues back to grab the mag rifle. Jimmy rolls up his suit and pats Dixon on the shoulder, smiling.

"Couple of mag rifles help you boys out?" Gizmo says as he reaches for the gun. "New addition to the armoury since your days, Dixon." He hands it over. Dixon takes a hold and is instantly impressed at how light it feels. Its design reminiscent of an old AK-47, but with a bit bulkier. The barrel isn't a cylinder either, four prongs stretch out with a compensator at the end that comes to a sharp point. He turns it in his hand several times.

"You know, I uh-" Gizmo's tone turns serious "I'm sorry about what happened to you, Dixon. Real shame about your two angels." Dixon turns his eyes to Gizmo, they soften a little as he talks.

"I may not get out of here much but I remember seeing you, your girls and Sadie at the park. I always liked you lot, probably one of the only glimmers of something beautiful left in this world. If I had the strength, I'd be out of this chair hunting down the fuckers that did that to you. I'd take every weapon I've got here and use it on them." His cracked lips quiver a little. Dixon does his best to hold it together, resting a hand on Gizmo's shoulder.

"Thanks, Giz. Sadie always liked hearing the stories of the old days you had to tell. I know the girls would have too". A lump forms in Dixon's throat. He pauses, and the two of them share a look of understanding. "Now tell me about this thing" he cocks the gun back in his hands.

Gizmo shakes his head and takes a deep breath. "Lightweight, quiet and super-efficient. If you've got a problem with how this thing handles, then the problem is you!" He grabs the gun from Dixon, placing it in his lap, gripping the handle, he flicks a switch on the side of the gun and an LCD window flickers on with "0000" displayed. Gizmo points it at Dixon.

"This baby has multiple fire settings; single, burst, auto and turbo. Flick it up to turbo and she'll spit out nine hundred needles in around fifteen seconds." He tilts it to the side, popping the empty clip off easily. "Each clip holds around fifteen hundred needles, so if you do decide to paint a target with holes, keep in mind you'll be out quick."

"So why don't we take a railgun? Used that trusty beast against the riots when Halo wiped out that little village. Worked a treat" Dixon says remembering the rebellious locals who wouldn't budge. The railgun tearing through the buildings they stayed in, while also keeping anyone close by firmly in their shit stained spot.

"He's right, Dix. We don't want to go in guns blazing. That's too loud. If Lopez has elite Talons guarding him, then he'll be able to get a hold of back up easily" Jimmy reassures him.

"Railgun - you'll blow out the walls and ears of everyone in the building. Mag rifle - you'll be able to wipe out a guy's insides through three walls and nobody will hear a thing." Gizmo leans back into his chair, perching his chin on his fist.

"Wipe out?" Dixon asks

Jimmy takes the gun, plugs the clip back in, winks at Dixon. "Incapacitate" He walks further up the aisle and grabs a couple of LAF issue combat blades, tossing one to Dixon. "You got another mag rifle for me that won't be missed?"

Gizmo stops and raises up to a standing position. "Gentlemen, the last time I saw somebody down here, it was two rookies who were gearing up to go out for a raid in the gallows. One big ugly fuck" he looks at Dixon. "And one scrawnier, slightly less ugly prick." He looks at Jimmy. "As far as I'm concerned this is all pretty much your stuff. Just leave chuck alone." Gizmo disappears back into the room he emerged from. Dixon, curious, shouts after him.

"Chuck?" As his voice echoes, he hears a gruff noise. A slow paced pat rings through the silence before a wrinkled and old looking St Bernard peeks out of the doorway. It tilts its head at the sight of Dixon, spotting Jimmy it pants a little.

"Hey Chuck" Jimmy locates another mag rifle under a table, rolls it up in his suit and carries it over his shoulder as he walks away. Dixon follows after Jimmy, looking back at the dog, tilting its head again, it lets out a faint growl of curiosity.

"C'mon Chuck!" Gizmo's voice shouts. Chuck turns from the doorway and paws off, the door slamming shut behind him.

Chapter 13

"No, he's not LAF assigned," Jimmy says to Dixon, before he can ask the question. "Giz found the pup not long after you left. The poor little guy was hiding in the trash behind the precinct. Must have been running from a mod gang wanting him for fights."

The two of them ascended the stairs and quickly ducked into the staff toilets. Grotty looking, and as abused as Dixon remembered, they spend little time hanging around. Grabbing a stall each and undressing so they can put on the valk-suits.

"The modders use the dogs for fights?" Dixon asks, over the cubicle partition.

"Yup. They jab them and malnourish them so that they get desperate and angry. Toss them in a pit with another poor dog and let them fight it out till one is dead. Thousands of credits get bet on them. Even some high levellers have been spotted at events." Jimmy explains.

"Sick fucks!" says RJ. Dixon slaps his arm chastising her.

"Yeah, it's messed up. Not as messed up as when they take the torn up dogs away after the fight, juice them up with adrenaline and mod the dogs. Replace limbs and teeth, almost giving them weapons instead. Eventually, there are too many machine parts and not enough dog left, and it gives out."

"Bastards!" RJ and Dixon say together.

Covering themselves again in their regular clothes, and exiting, they check how they look in the mirrors.

Adjusting his shoulders and neck, Jimmy remarks, "Not too bulky, heavy though".

"We'll get used to them," Dixon says, as he checks his edges, making sure it doesn't look too obvious.

Jimmy kinks his mouth left to right. "Feels almost like its itching, and like I should be sweating my balls off in this thing." Dixon turns and nudges him out of the bathroom.

"That's just because you've never had the build for clothing to stretch around you" He laughs as they leave the precinct and head back towards Jimmy's car.

"Alright ass-wipe, not everyone was born with your freakishly broad shoulders and frame. I had to work to get in this shape." Jimmy laughs as he pretends to flex his muscles under his leather jacket. He wasn't a scrawny man. Jimmy saw it more as a benefit, a hidden strength. "I'm surprised you're so large still, thought all that destroying yourself would have left you a quivering stack of bones".

"Hmm," Dixon reaches the car, opens the door and slides in "that was probably one of the things that kept me sane. Working out while shit faced gave me an angry focus and a stupid lack of control." He looks down at his hands, cracking his knuckles. "Too drunk to know when to stop."

As Jimmy turns the key, and the engine whirrs to life, his arm chirps. He pulls his sleeve back and sees a notification alert. Pulling the sleeve back down, he taps a display on the dashboard and a holo-display syncs with his arm. Dixon leans over to get a better look.

"What's up?" he asks.

"Sadie's quick! She's sent through a bunch of files already" Jimmy says surprised.

"Great. We can look them over on the way to Chester's." Dixon clenches his fists feeling the armour grip his forearms tightly. He wonders if he could flex through it like he had done with t-shirts when Sadie started dating him. Thinking again he realises, there was no chance he'd be strong enough to break it.

They roll off from the precinct. Jimmy sets the destination into the car's dashboard and hits the auto-drive. The steering wheel slowly peels back into the dashboard, the gear stick folds down allowing both of them to adjust into a more relaxed position. Jimmy begins filtering down the files received after skimming through the first three. Dixon watches him work away, remembering how much of a stickler for detail he used to be.

"Need any help?" Dixon grumbles. Fully aware of the response he'll get.

"Uh, nope. I'm good man" Jimmy says, a dead silence fills the car for five seconds, and then Jimmy raises his head seeing Dixon's mild frustration. "Come on man, this was how we used to work. You did the heavy lifting and physical force, and I did the pencil pushing." He smiles supportively.

"Sat there and looked pretty you mean?" Dixon looks from the corner of his eye, edging a sneer.

"Give Sadie a call, maybe she can give us some tips," Jimmy says, peeling his sleeve back and flicking through a couple of menus. Tapping twice on his arm before burying his head back into the files.

"New contact received" RJ pipes up from Dixon's arm. "Sadie Knight, hmm. Please don't go getting drunk and trying to phone her at three in the morning".

A faint digital sigh emanates from his arm before RJ recalls. "Remember that time I had to call an ambulance because you'd pissed and vomited yourself unconscious while sobbing outside the house you two used to..."

"Shut up and call her!" Dixon thumbs at his arm harshly. RJ's voice cutting off and the call initiating, Sadie's name displayed in green with a pulsating circle around it. It pulses four times and then cuts out.

RJ's voice returns. "No connection available. And I might add, cutting me off is rather ru...". Dixon pushes the call button again, but the display simply pulses four times again and cuts out.

"I swear you're either pissed at Sadie, or pissed at me. Just don't cut me off, would you?" RJ moans. Dixon ignores her.

"Can't get through, she must be in hiding." Says Dixon.

"Smart move, if Halo finds out she's been snooping they'll go fuck shit crazy," says Jimmy as he leans back, still focused on the files. "There are four transactions about to go through, and two that passed yesterday that could relate to this merger."

"Huh?" Dixon shakes his head.

"Look" he warps the holo-display larger for them both to see. "These two properties were transferred from Fenghuang to Halo for next to nothing. They are close to Feng HQ in China."

He swipes through to other files. "And these four are for property going the other way. The two in China are listed as new research and manufacturing sites for Halo. The other four properties, from Halo going to Feng, have perfect tactical advantage for a potential military force to control the entirety of Colorado."

"What are you thinking?" Dixon asks.

"Well, if the merger goes through, then Fenghuang is going to have what looks like two of the biggest research labs ever next to their home, and Halo is going to have perfect staging grounds for a military force to take control of everyone. Both Colorado and North Eastern China would become totally secure to them." Jimmy raises his eyebrows. "Stronghold fortresses like that would make it pretty damn easy to push rival territories back."

"Let's see what Chester thinks" Dixon nods.

Chapter 14

Driving past the front door of Chester's building, they turn down an alley. Rubbish and abandoned goods fly up as the car edges down the narrow corridor. Pulling into a small loading dock for an abandoned shop, the two exit the vehicle. A homeless man with an implanted eye wakes, and looks over at them. Dixon motions for him to remain calm, and the eye turns from yellow to blue. The homeless man shakes his head and mumbles some insult, before turning over and returning to sleep.

They sneak along the alleyway, taking the back route to the building, as they reach it Dixon leans against the wall, poking his head out slightly to check if the coast is clear. Jimmy leans against the wall, standing behind Dixon.

"What d'you see?" Jimmy asks.

"Looks clear, oh, wait," Dixon notices one of the talon guards stepping out from a doorway and looking down either direction of the alley. "One elite, what's the approach?"

"Spare change?" Jimmy asks as Dixon looks back at him. The two nod.

"I've got a very bad feeling about this" RJ says.

They shimmy out into the alleyway in plain sight of the talon guard. His head quickly turns to face them, the lights on his helmet focusing on them for identification. The built-in computer processing them in its digitised voice.

"Two men approach, facial recognition – no result. Statistical analysis enabled. Covered in rags, slumped posture, sloppy footing. Homeless? Highly likely. Inebriated? Highly likely" The talon hears in his helmet. He turns his body to face them.

The mumbles slowly get closer before Dixon speaks up. "Hey, you, Mr, uh, Mr, spare any change for a poor bum" The words not seeming to land with the guard, who reaches into his suit and pulls out a thick rod.

"Back up" The talon orders. Raising a hand as the two continue to close the distance.

"I repeat, back up!" A firmer tone emanates from the helmet with a metallic tone. The guard whips the rod in his hand, it extends further, and arcs of electricity begin shooting up and down it.

As they close in even closer, the guard reaches into his jacket again with his free hand, pulling out a matte black pistol. A gold phoenix leers down the barrel, a gold blade attached to the top and bottom of it shimmers in the light. "Back the fuck up you bums, or this is going to be your worst day"

"Really?" Dixon's voice breaking from the rasp he put on, to clear arrogance. Both Dixon and Jimmy whip their rags off. They fly into the air as the mag rifles emerge into the light. Within a second both are aimed at the guard. He tries to quickly draw the pistol up to them, but it is too late.

He drops to his knees, as a faint ting is heard in the distance. A small puncture in his suit begins to spit out blood in a rapid stream. A small hole in the helmet also pours red down the smooth black. The faucet of blood from his chest slows down as he falls to the ground. Jimmy looks to Dixon who is almost gasps.

"Fuck me!" Dixon looks at the gun and then back at the disposed of guard, the compensator at the end of Dixon's mag rifle fizzing as the hot metal singes the dust particles around it. Jimmy's gun doesn't fizzle. Looking back at the gun Dixon smiles. Flapping the remaining rags off his arm, he opens the door the guard was protecting and looks back at Jimmy. "C'mon, Kersh" he beckons.

"Think he had any family?" Jimmy asks, staring at the body as it leaks. Dixon reaches to him and pulls him inside, shaking Jimmy back to attention.

"I think we need to get to Chester Lopez and make him spill the details." Dixon edges to a corner inside the corridor, checking the coast is clear again. He looks back to Dixon who slowly walks behind him. "Besides, I bet the guy didn't even have a girlfriend, was probably cooked up in some geek lab somewhere". Jimmy nods and cocks his rifle.

"Yeah, just never killed anyone" explains Jimmy.

"Seen plenty of corpses though" Dixon squares up to Jimmy.

"I've seen dead people, people beating the shit out of each other, hell, I watched you obliterate the face of the guy we're about to go and see. I've never seen someone die though." Jimmy looks up at Dixon, showing the truth in his statement. Dixon stares back for a couple of seconds before blinking and rolling a shoulder.

"Forgot you weren't at White River when all that shit went down" He manages to stifle a half smile before turning and leading the way around the corner. The corridor is tiled and littered with storage boxes. Eventually, they reach a large metal door with a circular window in it. Peering through, Dixon reports back.

"Kitchen!" The two nod at each other and edge through. People work away not noticing them, the head chef chopping away at some meat, too mangled to decipher. Dixon quickly sneaks up behind him, gun pointed directly at the back of his head he taps his right shoulder. The chef turns around, his rotund figure nearly pushing Dixon away. As he sees both men he inhales sharply, the notices Jimmy with his LAF badge on display. A finger to his lips, he softly shushes the chef.

Grunting and frowning in return, the chef turns back, mumbling in an unknown language and pointing to the door. Jimmy relaxes a little and looks to Dixon. Both shrug and walk calmly through the kitchen, staff paying little attention apart from stepping out of their way and trying not to drop dishes.

They push through the next set of doors - another corridor. To the right are a set of stairs and the three elevators that Jimmy and Dixon used on their first visit. To the left - the restaurant area of the building. Dixon scoffs as he peers through the window in the door. Several couples sit in large comfortable looking booths, extravagant meals and drinks spread across their tables. Waiters dressed to the nines provide any and every service they can to get a coin thrown their way. It's dark, but Dixon can make out the sharp eyes of two talon guards at the back of the restaurant area. No doubt there are two standing on the other side of the door.

Jimmy signals the elevator, and it swoops quietly - the doors parting they slip in and press Chester's floor. Jimmy breathes a little easier once the doors close.

"You were put on White River as a special assignment. You had the better marksmanship scores, and they needed me filling the database back then. How many was it?" Jimmy doesn't look over to Dixon as he asks. In his peripheral vision he sees Dixon sigh and box his head. It feels like an eternity passes before Dixon speaks.

"Two thousand" He swallows, and looks off into space, remembering the slaughter. LAF was called in to support Halo ground forces during a rush of people from Utah. Rumours had come in of anti-Halo terrorists and Fenghuang collaborators. Orders were to oversee and diffuse potential situations. When they arrived Halo troops had already been overrun; the arrogance of Halo to put twenty rookies with no field experience out there. Dixon's commanding officer quickly rallied his squad, screaming to open fire on the crowd of colours and voices hurtling at them. Bullets tore through flesh and muscle. Within ten minutes the scene resembled an old war battlefield.

That was the first time that Dixon received prescribed time away from work. The majority of the squad suffered from PTSD; when they rolled the bodies over, they discovered the majority of the crowd were women and children. A few elderly males were also amongst them, a crowd of people who were in actuality, fleeing from the oppressive hardness of Salt Lake City.

"Eighty-Second Floor" The plain voice stated, as the elevator arrived at its destination. Dixon blinking and bringing the rifle up to aim, the doors slide open and both look cautiously at the empty hallway. Poking their heads out, they see no guards, and exit the elevator, this time knowing the correct route to take to Chester's place. They work their way around slowly, checking corners and covering each other. Finally, they come to the corner, looking around at Chester's door and seeing two talon's on either side of it.

"Shit!" Dixon whispers.

"Don't think we can pull a spare change on this one," Jimmy winces. "What are we going to do?" They move back down the corridor a bit, to consider.

As they mull over possible ideas, Dixon suddenly feels a buzz in his thigh. Not pain but a tingle, shortly after, a thump on his head puts him to his knees. Jimmy darts a look down the corridor where they came from. A talon races towards them, having thrown a heavy mace like device at Dixon, realising that his energy pistol had little effect.

Jimmy grabs Dixon's shoulder, pushing him to the ground and leaning against him as he reels the gun up and sprays needle hellfire in the guard's direction. The walls shred as the needles pass through. The guard falls to his knees as he pours blood from the fresh holes, his hand holding the pistol almost falling off from the tear it now has in it. Jimmy sighs, breathing with a sense of relief.

"Two more coming," RJ says, as Dixon grunts in pain at the throbbing in the side of his head. Jimmy whips around to see the two guards covering the door turn the corner to investigate the thump of the body hitting the floor. Jimmy shreds through them as they jump in realisation of their fate. This time Jimmy's aim is a little more focused than his first spray. A gush of blood comes from the first guard's chest as he rag dolls to the ground. The other takes a few needles to the face. His helmet getting torn to pieces, revealing a chunk of his face and neck missing, blood pouring down his body, he joins his colleague on the floor.

Dixon pulls himself up, rubbing his head and neck. "Good job buddy, that fucker came out of nowhere". He pats Jimmy, thanking him. Rising to his feet, he steps over the two bodies. "You coming?"

"Right behind you," Jimmy says, catching his breath from the adrenaline coursing through his veins, the spray of blood on the walls shaking his nerves a little. He manages to regain focus and joins Dixon at the door. Both stand either side, Dixon readies himself before knocking on the door. Murmurs of a disgruntled voice get louder before the door opens.

"I thought I was crystal fucking cle…". Before Chester can finish, a mag rifle is pressed firmly against his forehead. He pauses, springs his hands in the air, dropping the glass from his hand. It bumps on the carpet and spills the rum, staining it a dark golden.

Dixon pushes him back into the apartment with his gun, Chester trying his best not to stumble as he backs into the living room. Jimmy quickly follows, closing the door and assessing each room he enters. Quickly moving from room to room, Dixon waits and stares Chester dead in the eye. His trembling lip the only movement between the two of them.

"Clear" Jimmy says, returning from upstairs. His gun lowered and his smile returned. Visibly restored to his original. Dixon relaxes his grip on the gun a little and takes a step back.

"Miss me?" Dixon says, he can see the terror in Chester's eyes.

"Wh-what do you want?" Chester asks. Their entrance into the apartment had been so quick and controlled, that neither Dixon nor Jimmy had noticed his face.

"Fixed your mouth up a bit huh?" Dixon says, while inspecting the new origin of Chester's slightly digitised voice. No nose remains at all, his mouth a bizarre mixture of flesh and tendons wrapped around shining chrome metal. It's not a working jaw but more like a sculpture of one, set in place. Two holes are centred where the mouth once was, one with a grating over it, the other dripping a small remnant of rum. A slight beehive like dome replaces the nose almost looking like an old style car exhaust, eight slits of vents emitting his breath.

"I can't eat anything now, I'm sucking through a straw thanks to you" Chester's eyes lower. Clearly the change in his facial structure putting a downer on the rest of his days.

Jimmy peers round, scowls his face in disgust. "Bet you are a shit kisser now too". He steps aside and leans on the arm of the sofa opposite. Dixon sits down at the other end of the sofa, propping his feet up on the table, gun still firmly squared.

"Needed some protection, did you? Can't blame you for being a little scared I guess" Dixon says "I've got to say, I'm very impressed at how you managed to get elite talons guarding you".

"I, uh, I'm an important guy at Fenghuang. I deal with big accounts." Chester says, speaking to the floor.

"Bullshit! Elites only go to the top dogs of Feng, you may be hot shit, but you certainly aren't top dog material" Dixon leans forward.

"They look out for their employees" Chester reasons.

"They might for the top dogs like he said" Jimmy butts in. "But after you got a glory hole and vibrator strapped to your face, you aren't ever making it to executive." Dixon's eyes don't hesitate, fixed on Chester's, they almost inflict pain with their intensity.

"Look, Dixon"

"Oh, so you *do* remember me?" Dixon smiles a little.

"I do, now. Brought up your file when I was in the hospital. I get it. You're pissed at me I killed your daughters" As Chester explains, Dixon's famous grimace crawls onto his face a little, pushing Chester deeper into the seat.

"I may be an asshole for that. You don't want to mess with these guys though." says Chester.

"The documents I saw upstairs, explain," says Dixon, nodding at the office upstairs.

"Legal shit I have to take care of. The execs put it in place, but wanted it kept hush hush. Nobody tracks paper these days - but it's still official. I'm to take it to Halo to get it processed. Would have done before you came in and nearly put me in a coma." The digitised voice breaking from his natural tone occasionally. The implant must not be great at dealing with a lack of breath.

"Who is it going to at Halo?" Jimmy asks.

"I don't know, some bitch called Leanne Watkins." Jimmy looks to Dixon as Chester reveals the lead. Dixon doesn't break his stare. "Her receptionist set up the appointment the day you attacked me. Hey, wait. Isn't she...". As Chester connects the dots and points to Dixon, a loud crash explodes from the door. Smoke billows out of the entrance corridor. Jimmy and Dixon quickly stand and spin round, fixing their guns on the cloud growing. Dixon grabs Chester and throws him into a chokehold in front of him. He hesitates a little, as the far smaller man sputters spit and strange noises, while he chokes.

"Drop your weapons" A loud metallic voice states. Dixon fires a look at Jimmy.

"Drop your weapons, now!" the voice rings again. Neither move. Gunfire suddenly springs out of the cloud, painting the kitchen area and shattering three of the large glass windows. Jimmy ducks behind a table as Dixon throws himself and Chester behind a sofa. Three talons appear from the smoke, each one holding an energy rifle. One has a nine-inch blade, another a baton spitting out electricity, and the last one a katana strapped to his back. They scan the room, not noticing the men due to the mess their blind fire caused.

The man with the baton quickly goes upstairs. The other two spread out, one looking around the kitchen area and moving toward the bathroom. The other slowly edges around the living room. He moves closer and closer to the sofa Dixon and Chester hide behind.

"Documents secured" the voice of the guard upstairs echoes down.

"Hey!" Chester manages to call out between the strong grips of Dixon's arm around his neck. The talon quickly adjusting his gun, points it at the sofa. Dixon grunts.

"Shit" He quickly throws Chester out of the way, hoping for the talon to take the bait. He doesn't; looking quickly at Chester and then back to the sofa.

"Fuck" Dixon shouts again as he springs from hiding as the talon lights up the sofa with energy. It bursts into flames and splits in two. Dixon quickly side steps as the talon brings his gun around to shoot again, releasing an energy charge out of the window. The baton swinging quickly in and smashes off Dixon's hip, the energy dissipating over the armour which takes the brunt of the hit. Dixon needs only to correct his stance slightly before Dixon grabbing the talon's arm with the baton and swinging it down between his legs. A gulp of pain can be heard, followed by a scream, as the talon feels the voltage through his genitals. Dixon brings his mag rifle to the chin of the man and pulls the trigger. A needle flies straight up through the ceiling and into the floor above. The body instantly goes limp and falls to the floor.

"Fuck!" Chester shouts as he witnesses the execution. The guard checking the bathroom sprints out to see the situation - only to be dump tackled by Jimmy. The two tussle over control, before Jimmy manages to elbow his arms free, mashing the butt of his rifle into the helmet, dazing the talon but not eliminating him. He grabs for the blade strapped to his leg and pulls it free, swiping at Jimmy in one go. Missing he adjusts the blade in his hand to stab back in the other direction. Jimmy drops the rifle and manages to catch the blade. Straddled on top of him, he turns the blade downward and leans all of his weight on top. The blade slowly descends towards a crack in the talons helmet as he loses his strength, Frustration coming from the talon as he struggles against his demise. Finally, the blade enters the helmet and he struggles no more.

Dixon pulls Chester to his feet as Jimmy leans back, still straddling the body, breathing in exhaustion. Dixon squints at Chester, smashing the butt of the mag rifle into the car exhaust nose of his face. His head springs back accompanied by an audible yelp. Jimmy pats himself down, making sure he has no injuries.

"Did you see how many there were?" Jimmy asks, slowly rising to his feet.

Dixon reels the gun back, ready to hit Chester again. Just as he is about to thrusts it forward, he notices a faint curling in Chester's brow. A flicker of light momentarily blinds Dixon, his mag rifle dropping out of his grip and hitting the floor. Noticing a sharp feeling in his arm he looks at the display, normally he'd see RJ's sarcastically smiling emoticon face. Instead, the display has a perfectly straight cut through it. Confused Dixon looks closer, the cut isn't just through the device but through his entire arm. He tries to turn his wrist, but the limb falls from him. Floods of blood pour from the stump just below the elbow. His forearm thumps to the ground and rests against his feet.

Dixon turns to see the third talon holding his katana aloft, a small drop of blood dripping from it. Still unaware of the pain beginning to throb through his arm, Dixon quickly throws a fist in the talons direction. The man swats his punch away with the side of his sword. Dixon tries to punch with his now stumped arm, the man punches it back. His fist connecting with the bloody stump, Dixon wrenches back as the pain finally devours his brain. The talon whirls the katana around to his back, squatting down as he grabs the energy pistol.

In one graceful manoeuvre, the guard shoots into the air, spinning a full circle and kicking Dixon in the face before landing and ploughing two energy charges directly into his chest. Dixon falls back from the force and shouts furiously in pain. Clutching at his arm.

Stepping over and standing above Dixon, the guard holsters his gun and twirls the katana up above his head. Pointed directly down he bounces to his tiptoes before growling, about to plant the blade in Dixon's chest.

A faint flutter rings from the kitchen as the man stalls in a pose. The blade shatters and darts off, landing on the floor. As Dixon looks up, he can see what looks like bolts of blood shooting from the man's back. Quickly followed by chunks of flesh exploding off his body. Finally his body folds backwards, the spine letting off a sharp crack as it splits.

Dixon leans up, seeing the ruin of viscera laid before him. Looking back, he sees Jimmy holding his mag rifle pointed in his direction, the compensator glowing bright white from unloading the entire clip. Jimmy's face is a picture of shock and surprise.

"So that's what turbo fire is like" Jimmy mutters. He leans around the corner looking for Dixon's usual sardonic grin of approval, instead seeing the lopped off arm and contorting a Dixon holding his stump. Jimmy tosses the gun down.

"Fuck, buddy, you ok?" He props Dixon up on his knee, listening to him hide his pain beneath the angry growls.

"Little shit was fast. Thanks for taking him out before he made me a kebab". Dixon grunts out, amidst the surges of pain, the colour dropping from his face quickly. He shifts his focus to getting up, grabbing his gun from the floor and kicking the corpse that attacked him. Jimmy darts to the kitchen and grabs several cloths, creating a makeshift tourniquet as best he can.

"Holy shit" Chester stands up from his squatted, quivering hiding spot, looking at the carnage laid out across his apartment. Dixon begins edging down the entrance corridor, leaving palm prints of blood. Jimmy grabs Chester and shoves him down the corridor as well.

As Dixon approaches the door Chester sees the grim stump dripping blood. "Buddy, you are fucked up". Dixon looks back at him, a pale face still booming rage, his eyes dulling as he struggles to remain conscious. Realising he can't hold himself much longer, Dixon summons all the remaining energy he has and reels the gun up. Jimmy quickly leaps out of the way as Dixon pulls the trigger. Chester falls to the ground with a small and perfect hole in the centre of his forehead. Looking down at his body, Dixon breathes slower, lowering the gun to Chester's face and pulling the trigger four more times before finally succumbing, and hitting the ground hard. Jimmy looks at the two of them lying in the corridor and at the men in the room. He is the only man left standing on this floor of the building.

Chapter 15

Regaining consciousness in a blur of confusion, Dixon lunges up, pointing the mag rifle at the first figure he sees. Holding his arm as best he can, if a bit shakily, he blinks, clearing his vision, the figure reveals itself, Jimmy stands looking back with a smile of relief. Dixon lowers his arm, realising now that he also doesn't have his mag rifle.

He looks around, lying in a bed, still wearing his boots, jeans and shirt but his jacket is gone. A throb of a headache reminds him of what transpired. He wasn't hungover, this pain wasn't as bad as some of the hangovers he'd had. Running his hand across his head he wonders where he is.

"Jimmy?" He asks, still looking around the dark room.

"We're at the nearest stitcher I could find." Jimmy rests his hands at the end of the bed. "Thought you'd lost too much of your juice to come back. You're pretty tough to kill, you know?" Jimmy says, hiding the choked up feeling in his throat.

Dixon frowns as he squints, focussing his vision as best he can. The room is tiled like a hospital surgery, but this is too dark to be a professional environment like that. It appears clean enough, but the back of the room suggests a seedier tone. Fake body parts hang on a wall like an armoury's selection of weapons. Posters litter the walls near the entrance to the room. Seeing the staircase through the doorway, Dixon understands fully where he is.

"A god damn stitcher, Jimmy?" Dixon flexes as he starts to lean up. Jimmy raises his arm to calm him.

"Dix, don't get up, you're going to want to stay lying down for a bit." Jimmy circles around the bed, resting his hands on Dixon's chest, halting him. "I know you don't like these guys but the nearest hospital is twenty miles away. You'd have bled out long before we got there. Besides, this guy's got a good range of stock." Jimmy looks down at Dixon's arm.

Dixon suddenly remembers losing his arm. He twitches his fingers on his left arm, they move. He can feel some adjusting movement, but it isn't the same as he is used to. Raising his arm, his eyes widen sharply in awe. A prosthetic arm extends from the stump, partially carbon fibre, partially titanium in its core. The parts that aren't exposed to see the inner workings, are covered by expensive looking white material. Replicating the look of muscles it is lined in blue, wrapping around the stump and up towards the elbow. Dixon notices the logo at the wrists.

"Halo" he grits his teeth, then laughs through his frustration. "Isn't that ironic" he looks to Dixon.

"I spent a good chunk of my retirement fund on that for you. It's top of the line" Jimmy's face twitches nervously. "At least you don't have a cheeky Irish girl giving you a hard time?"

"RJ?" Dixon looks back to his arm, noticing now that he doesn't have the display staring back at him. "What happened to her?"

Jimmy lowers his head, "She got chopped in two with your arm. Her processing unit and storage device were ruined. There's no way to retrieve her. She's gone."

Dixon grabs his Halo arm with his right hand, his real hand, feeling the cold material, thinking he can feel his grip. Processing it as best he can he quickly realises he is only having phantom feelings in a ghost arm. He suppresses a gasp of emotion as he thinks of RJ. Hurt that he'd lost his most attached friend, literally, and surprised as he comprehends just how much he really cared for an artificial intelligence.

He might not have felt so strongly for the AI, had he not named it after his daughters. Had the AI not taken on so much of his own personality when she returned after he left the LAF, he wouldn't have felt this loss. A loss edging so close to the loss of his two actual daughters. It hadn't crossed his mind that RJ had taken on his personality in the same fashion you would see children take on characteristics of their parents. Somehow RJ had taken on the smart wit that Sadie had. She really was like Rose and Jenny put together in a digital mashup and implanted into his arm. Dixon sniffs and blinks back the tears he wants to shed. Jimmy nods in understanding.

"I'll go get the doc," he says turning and exiting up the stairs.

Dixon takes a deep breath and does his best to push the feelings deep down inside, like he has done his entire life. Forcing himself to use the arm and learn how much control he has; opening the hand and closing it into a fist, after a minute he links his fingers with it, closing the grip and feeling how strong it actually is. A tear creeps out and runs down his cheek.

Gripping harder he feels the raw strength the arm has. Nearly crushing every bone in his remaining hand. He releases the grip and shakes the pain out before wiping the tear from his face.

"Ah! I see you're getting to grips with it quite literally" A foreign accent comes from the doorway. Dixon looks over to see Jimmy enter with the 'doctor', presumably.

"I am Frederick Richter," The man says taking up a spot at one side of the bed, Jimmy standing opposite.

"Doctor?" Dixon asks.

"I was, a former brain surgeon in western Germany before Fenghuang ran me out" His German accent amplifying his contempt for the company. "However my specialist surgical credentials are not recognized here. I'd have to spend ten years learning Halos techniques of medicine." Rolling his r's, his tone lightens. "I've spent the better part of my life dedicated to medicine, I'd rather help the common man than their executive ranks."

Dixon leans up from the bed, moving each finger individually. "Well, you fixed my arm and stopped me from losing all my human juice. We'll call you, doc" Dixon smiles as he looks at Jimmy and the doctor. Jimmy nods approvingly.

"Thank you, gentlemen" the doctor walks away from the bed, tapping his fingertips together. "The arm needs roughly two weeks of physical therapy and adjustment to become second nature to you. I suspect you gentlemen don't have that kind of time to waist."

"Not wrong there, doc," Jimmy says.

"Well, as long as you take care with it while mashing gangs faces in, then you should be back to full working order within two months I'd say then." The doc links his fingers and rests his arms in front of himself.

Dixon looks at Jimmy, shrugs and says "Works for me. I can still pull a trigger" he winks.

"Wunderbar!" The doctor smiles. "My work appears to be done for now then gentlemen. I'll give you the room for twenty minutes to collect yourselves and your things. I have an appointment coming in after that by, which time you will have to be gone."

"No problems, doc" Jimmy thanks the doctor with a salute. Dixon nods, and the doctor exits up the stairs.

Jimmy turns to Dixon as the footsteps from the stairs get quieter. "So, after you plugged Chester" Dixon smiles as he recalls the moment, "I swiped these". Jimmy reaches into his jacket and pulls out the folder containing the paper legal documents, the Fenghuang and Halo logos on the front. Dixon's eyes light up again, he swivels off the bed and grabs the folder. Splotches of blood stain the folder and have seeped into the pages. Dixon flicks through them as his smile grows.

"Beautiful" Dixon remarks.

"While you were out, I tapped into LAF, there's something else, Dix," Jimmy says, getting serious again.

"Huh?" Dixon turns to Jimmy.

"The database has flagged up a potential threat to Sadie as well. Apparently, Halo noticed her poking around and lingering on files. They've issued a warrant for her." Jimmy looks at Dixon in concern.

"A warrant? She must have got out and made a run for it. Where would she go?" Dixon's face breaking from its usual rock like expression.

Jimmy ponders for a few seconds. "She's a smart cookie, she probably bolted as soon as she sent the files."

Dixon rises from the bed, holding his arm with some care as he extends it. Checking the range of motion, his face cringes a little at the stiffness and slight pain he feels. He tosses the file to Jimmy and grabs his jacket. Gripping the collar and throwing the jacket around himself, Dixon pushes his arm down the sleeve like he's done a thousand times from muscle memory.

Jimmy giggles under his breath as Dixon's arm misses the sleeve of the jacket and folds as he tries to adjust it. His elbow instead goes into the sleeve first. Dixon stops for a second, trapped in his jacket, and looking at Jimmy - entirely unimpressed. He manages eventually to shrug the jacket off his arm and slip the sleeve on. He pulls it tightly around himself and checks his arm again.

Jimmy walks over to the staircase with a comical butler pose, bowing and gesturing up the stairs. Dixon nudges him as he passes.

"Ooh, he puts on a jacket!"

Chapter 16

Leaving the stitcher's shop, Dixon looks around, realising they were only a couple of blocks over from Chester's building, and into an alleyway. Formerly the Chinatown area of the city, it had since become a bit of a slum neighbourhood, the odd shop dotted throughout the streets hidden under the cover of poverty-stricken homes. Black market weapons were rife through this area. Not much surprise that Fenghuang had situated one of their largest towers here for their staff and morally ambiguous people to live in.

Wasting no time in getting out of the area, Jimmy and Dixon were less focused on not getting shot by a passer-by, but more so on getting to wherever Sadie had fled.

"You know where she regularly goes?" Dixon asks.

"She's your ex-wife, man," Jimmy says trying to speed around traffic.

"Don't know if you noticed buddy, I've basically been in a drunk coma for the past few years." Says Dixon.

"You think she went home?" Jimmy says

"No, she's smarter than that. She'd know not to go there. That's the first place they'd go looking." Dixon tries to think, but gets lost in anger.

After a minute of silence while they two of them think Jimmy pipes up, "Ok, hang on". He paws at the display, a line fades into view and responds.

"Detective Kershon, how may I assist," a polite voice asks.

"Sadie Knight's address, give it to me." Jimmy's eyes don't leave the road as he swerves left and right around vehicles and crowds of shouting pedestrians.

"Sadie Knight, Apartment J, Apollo Gardens" The voice states clearly. Jimmy taps the display again and it fades to darkness.

"We don't have any other leads. We go there." Jimmy says. Dixon tries to think of an argument against it, finding nothing, he agrees.

Pulling into the neighbourhood where Sadie's building is situated, the comparison is almost night and day. Nine square blocks encapsulate the tower that Sadie stays in, and each of them looks like their own utopia. Large white buildings stretch to the clouds, some of them split in the middle, being held together by the elevators ascending through the gaps. Trees and exotic looking vegetation fill the gaps also, wrapped in ten-foot thick glass. Every amazing construction looking like some kind of spaceship that was waiting to launch into space.

Jimmy stops the car outside Sadie's building. They step out and immediately look at each other in shock, taking huge gulps of air as they realise that it almost tastes delicious. The pureness of everything around them bringing on a calm sense of joy. No wonder everyone walking around the area has a content smile fixed over their face.

They make their way to the building entrance, both with a slight gape on their faces. A couple of people nearly bump into them, but instead slow or stop in place to pass a polite welcoming pleasantry. Jimmy does his best to keep a somewhat fierce demeanour, expecting that they would have some trouble getting into the building, as they did with the Halo headquarters. Everyone else seemed to be wearing the standard Halo white and blue fashion, making them stick out like sore thumbs. Dixon alone stood out in most crowds thanks to his abnormal size. Strange, Jimmy felt, that after all the effort he himself put into looking good so he could stand out. Now he wished he could blend in.

"Good day, gentlemen. Please speak to our receptionist Jonie at the desk if you have any enquiries or appointments" A voice grabbed them. Spinning a couple of times they realise that the voice was coming from the building itself. No display with an AI face, no terminal, no drone, nothing for them to focus on. Instead, the entrance and walls themselves warped thin blue lines in accordance with the words. "Please, enter" it spoke again.

Walking in, they both notice how open this floor of the building is; almost entirely bare save for a few small seating areas and a bank of lifts and stairs on the right-hand side. To the left a desk with a tall smiling woman, seated, staring out like a spotlight.

"Gentlemen, welcome to Apollo Gardens, my name is Jonie. I'd be more than happy to help you with any questions you have while you are here." Her voice almost piercing in its attempt to be friendly. Dixon raises an eyebrow, every time he'd been spoken to like that it was either just before he got punched in the face or thrown out of the bar he was drinking in.

Jimmy smiles as best he can while feeling uncomfortable, noticing how attractive the woman is. Looking young and fresh-eyed, she couldn't have been older than twenty-three, her white hair perfectly straight sitting on her shoulders almost like a designer hood. Beaming blue eyes stared back with a similar shade on her plump lips.

"Hi, uh, Jonie." She turns to face Jimmy as he approaches and leans on the desk, doing his best to look cool. Her almost inhuman movements pushing Jimmy back off the desk, standing and putting his hands into his pockets awkwardly.

He shakes his nerves "I'm..."

"Detective Kershon, of the LAF" Jonie cuts him off, her smile wide like a puppet. Her eye implants circling blue digital designs.

"Right, and this is-"

"Dixon Callaway, formerly of the LAF. Ex-husband of Sadie Knight, who stays right here at Apollo Gardens". She flashes her smile in Dixon's direction. He turns his head away slightly, frowning at the young woman.

"Is that why you are here? To see Miss Knight? I can contact her right away and announce your arrival" Jonie's eyes drop behind the desk, her fingers furiously firing away at the keyboard.

"No, no, that's alright," Jimmy says, jumping back a little as Jonie locks her vision on him again. "If you could just tell us the floor she's on that would be great."

Jonie's head tilts a little bit. If she was actually a robot, this uncanny valley like creation could be about to break. Instead, her head springs back to its original position.

"It's a surprise" Dixon grumbles. Stepping closer to the desk, Jonie's head almost unhinges as she looks up.

She smiles wider "Certainly gentlemen. Simply take the far right lift at the bank back there, the building will do the rest."

Jimmy looks at the bank of lifts and spots the far right one mentioned. It's already open and waiting patiently. Nobody enters it, instead they all funnel into the other lifts and up the stairs. "Thank you, Jonie. Have a good day" Jimmy says, trying to flirt with a wink as he begins to walk off with Dixon. Jonie's eyes slowly swivel back to their default position.

"You think she's real?" Jimmy mumbles to Dixon.

"She certainly isn't normal," says Dixon.

"She is gorgeous though." Jimmy smiles, as they approach the lift.

"You're not normal either" Dixon mocks. They enter the lift and the doors close gently. A slight jolt hits them as the lift cabin launches up through the building, the glass chamber giving the full view as they ascend. They pass through a garden chamber and see small animal life living amongst the trees and bushes.

The chamber slows and halts at the floor with a friendly voice stating "Arrived at destination." They step out of the cabin and to another large hub like area. White walls, roof and ceiling surround them with the other lift tubes sitting in the middle of the room. Nobody is around and the silence is deafening as they look around, unaware of where to go. A light quickly shoots across the room from several directions. They culminate on the nearest wall and fade into a green blip, flashing slowly.

"Greeny!" Jimmy celebrates.

Dixon sighs and follows Jimmy and the lights, "Fuck!"

Jimmy's electronic friend leads them around to the other side of the floor and blips a few times at a door. He looks back at Dixon as they arrive, and gestures at the light as it fades.

"Get a girlfriend already," Dixon says, as he steps towards the door to Sadie's apartment. He knocks on the door and it swings open. The two look at each other, Jimmy pulling his pistol out of his holster, Dixon wishing he'd taken his mag rifle. Instead, he grimaces at his new arm, managing to ball a fist, the rubber fingertips creaking as it tightens. His other hand white with anticipation, they push open the door fully, and enter.

Jimmy leads with his pistol pointed steadily in front. The place isn't as big as Chester Lopez's, but is still of a decent size. The biggest difference from the Fenghuang accommodation is the minimalist look. A large living room caters to one white sofa and one white coffee table. Both would no doubt be facing the large window had they not been knocked over.

Jimmy quickly looks back to Dixon. "You check the right, I'll check left". Dixon nods and slides off to the right. A short corridor leads to a kitchen, the countertops only highlighted from the dazzling white by a blue outline. Drawers have been ripped open, cupboards nearly hang from their hinges and their contents have poured out onto the floor. Inching further down the corridor, Dixon finds the bathroom. Again a pure white room with toiletries, towels and cleaning products thrown about the place, the glass wall of the walk-in shower smashed along with the mirror above the sink.

Dixon exits the corridor again and checks the last door at the end, tossing open the door he finds a simple storage area. A couple of cleaning bots sit on the floor, one of them smashed to pieces. The shelves in the cupboard a mess of blankets and appliances. Finding nothing he turns and runs back in Jimmy's direction. Finding a large bedroom covered in clothes and nothing else he continues to the last room.

As he bursts into the room Jimmy whips his pistol up aiming at him. He exhales sharply and lowers his gun.

"Nearly put a hole in that ugly face of yours" He jokes, Dixon flips him the bird. He stands on the other side of a desk, Sadie's office looking more torn to pieces than the rest of the apartment. This room stands out more so due to the old furniture littered around.

"Almost feels like a secret den having all this old wood stuff around". Jimmy sifts through piles of personal belongings on the large table. Photobooks and picture frames catch his eye as he flips the chair over from the floor and sits down.

"She always did like old pieces like that," Dixon says, picking up an old chair that he remembers buying with Sadie a year after they were married. She found it at an old market, Dixon had no interest in going, but she managed to drag him along. Her charm held almost infinite power over him. He preferred the more relaxed sedentary lifestyle at that point; put on a movie with his wife and discuss who the worst actor was over a couple of bottles of wine. When Sadie wanted to go out and seek antiques like this Dixon couldn't refuse. Seeing her face light up as she blew the dust off of some old hunk of crap would always make Dixon smile. Just when Sadie thought she had swayed him into having an interest for it, they had their first child.

She saw very quickly that as soon as their little girl wrapped her hand around his giant finger, his heart had been stolen. He still loved Sadie as his wife, but this little bundle of cute smiles was his life now. With the arrival or the second girl not long after, Sadie had fallen in love all over again with the father that Dixon was. A giant beast of a man with the lightest touch for his two daughters. If they wanted to go and play in the garden, they would, for hours.

Dixon picks up one of the photo albums and sits down in the corner as he flicks through it. Memories of their first getaway flood back as he sees pictures of the beautiful beaches, their trip to Indonesia nothing short of a fantasy. The kind of pictures you'd see in holiday catalogues, the two of them entwined in each other's arms kissing or laughing littered the first few pages. As he thumbed further in he paused on one photo. Their wedding night, a large function hall with the light bouncing off the glitter ball above their head. The first dance they had as newlyweds. Dixon could almost hear the song playing in the back of his head. A piano performance by Gavin Degraw of his sombre toned "Belief". Dixon thought the song quite sad but Sadie showed her interest in the old song, remarking its "beautiful heartache".

Jimmy meanwhile, tapped his fingers away on the computer sitting at her desk. Impressed with the performance of such an old machine, Jimmy quickly realised that it had been upgraded with modern parts. Tied into the Halo network it performed without a microseconds pause. He grunts and leans back in the chair.

"Nothing" He shakes his head and looks over at Dixon in the corner. He still stares at the pictures in the book. Standing from the table Jimmy notices the page his eyes now fixate on. A picture of the entire family wrapped around each other, big grins and laughter fill the scene. Dixon lies on the ground in the garden with Sadie lying on top of him. Rose and Jenny trying to pounce on top of them from either side with childlike innocence.

"There's nothing here, buddy. Come on, let's go". Jimmy rests a hand on Dixon's shoulder, bringing him out of his daze. He turns his head up to Jimmy. He doesn't have the expression of angry pain that Jimmy had seen before when Dixon thought of his family, instead an almost defeated look of desolation peers back at him. He lowers his head to look at the picture again, slowly closing the photo album. He rests it on the desk and slowly rolls out of the chair. Adjusting his jacket he begins to leave the room.

"What now then?" He looks at Jimmy, hoping for the perfect solution.

"I don't know, she isn't here and it looks like they came looking for her." Jimmy looks around the rooms as they begin to exit the apartment. "I don't see any signs of a fight or struggle between people. Looks like they broke in and tried to find something - maybe information. She must have got away".

As they return to the corridors of the building Jimmy looks at the walls curiously.

"Where's greeny?" he asks.

"What? Oh, don't start with that shit, Kersh. I'm really not in the mood" says Dixon.

"No, I'm not joking, Dix. We should be getting shown out by that green blip, right? It isn't here" He continues looking around. Dixon realises he is right, and seeks the green blip. After a couple of seconds, the entire corridor fills with red. The strips where lights direct people on the walls glimmer red shooting off down the corridors. A siren begins to ring out across the entire floor.

"Ladies and gentlemen, please do not be alarmed. Remain in your homes while we lock the floor down. Security shall be here momentarily to resolve the situation." A powerful voice booms over the floor.

Jimmy looks to Dixon "Situation?"

"They must have rigged the system to flag when we arrive. Quick" Dixon sprints off down the corridor, Jimmy in pursuit.

The two peak round the corners as fast as they can, throwing themselves into the lift, the doors sliding closed behind them. Through the glass, Dixon can see someone trying to look out at the ruckus as his front door closes him back inside.

Dixon catches his breath as he wipes the sweat off his forehead. He may be as strong as he once was, but his cardio had never been fantastic, it was even worse now. "We've got to get this tube working," he says to Jimmy.

"On it!" Jimmy whips his sleeve back and brings up the display on his arm. He brings up the LAF database and puts in what seem like codes, followed by three-dimensional shapes. Looking up at the simple interface on the door he presses some buttons. They ripple distortion across the display, warps into a dark red cross a couple of times, before the entire display ripples a friendly green.

"Got it" Jimmy steps back with a proud grin on his face. "Tricked it into thinking we were residents who've been shot and need emergency evac."

"So you mean they're going to try and take us to the hospital when we get out of this thing?" Dixon asks as the lift descends.

"No dummy, the medical staff won't make it here before we leave. Besides, there may be enforcers waiting for us when we get out instead!" Jimmy's smile leaves his face as his tone gets serious.

"Great. I still don't have my mag rifle." Dixon curses.

"You've got the armour though, buddy. If Halo enforcers are down there they'll all be using energy weapons. We should be alright." Jimmy says reassuringly.

The lift reaches the bottom and the doors slide open. Nobody is walking into or out of the other lifts, nor is anyone climbing the stairs. Dixon edges out of the lift followed by Jimmy. Cautiously stepping across the floor, they begin to quicken their pace. Passing by the reception desk they break into a run. Jonie lifts and slowly swivels her head as they soar by.

"Good day gentlemen, have a pleasant day," She says as they exit. Looking down at her display - she sees a layout of the building with one floor flashing red. Pressing it, the display shows the notification of a security lockdown with pictures of Jimmy and Dixon's faces taken by the corridor cameras. She turns her head to look back out of the window. Luckily for them, they'd managed to jump into the car and escape her view.

She turns back to the display, still bearing her eerie smile.

Chapter 17

"That was close," Jimmy says, as a Halo squad unit hovers by at great speed, it's blue lights glimmering off the clean surfaces of the buildings and street. Dixon looks back to make sure they don't have a track on Jimmy's car.

"We have to find Sadie." Dixon pleads to Jimmy.

"Alright, look. Let's head back to your place. We'll gather everything together and try to figure out where she went, and what our next move is." Jimmy, managing to focus his brain, as Dixon still sheds off his emotional memories. He'd always known Dixon was an emotional person deep down inside. The years they served together would have taught him otherwise if he'd only seen him in a professional environment. A hard-edged cop with a bite worse than his bark. Meeting his family had shown Jimmy that even the roughest edges could hold some of the sweetest things.

Dixon rests in the chair, nodding a few times, mulling things over in his head. "Ok, yeah. Let's be rational", speaking to himself more than Jimmy. Dixon had always respected the restraint and control that Jimmy had in his work. While he may have regularly tried to get him to release his harder side, he knew that Jimmy held onto the concept of good police work. The only real moment Dixon could think of where Jimmy had stepped over the line of law and order, was letting him have his way with Chester. The laws of this world had changed, having a lot of shades of greys rather than blacks and whites. This grey line was what allowed Dixon to use his brash kind of police work, but he was fully aware that he wouldn't have been as effective without Jimmy's attention to detail.

They arrive at Dixon's flat, work their way up to his floor past the playing children and garbage and enter. Dixon picks up the pile of data cards from the hallway. The standard collection of flyer like advert cards. Plug them into your system and they'd bring up a flashy and catchy advert, normally filled with semi-naked women or obscenely attractive people. Dixon has relied on these for a while, thanks to their discount offers giving him his "first meal free".

Jimmy sits down at the table and brings up some of the files Sadie had sent to his arm display, checking them over for any further information. Dixon pours two drinks and hands one to Jimmy, he barely looks up to thank him, as he returns to the files. Dixon slowly swigs from the glass, enjoying the smoky burn in his throat as he sifts through the data cards.

Tossing them aside one by one; Thai, Indian, Italian and English. Each one brightly coloured, with the restaurant logo on it. Strip joint, strip joint, strip joint, another restaurant, strip joint and a Halo discount card. Dixon pauses, staring at the card. He rolls it over in his hand and notices a handwritten note. "DIXON, I'M SAFE" is written in block capital letters across it. He gulps down the whiskey and looks up.

"Jimmy" He walks around the table and sits down next to Jimmy, forcing the data card in front of his face. Jimmy's eyes dart over the writing and then shoot to Dixon.

"Plug it in!" Jimmy says hastily. Dixon slips the data card into a small box sitting on the coffee table. It fizzes a little and finally comes to life, after Dixon gives it a swift bash on the head, projecting a two-dimensional screen into the air, an image of a concerned Sadie looks back.

"Dixon, Jimmy. I found what you were looking for…" the view from just on top of her desk frames her, she looks up anxiously. "I'm sending it over to Jimmy's account. It'll be more secure under the LAF database. I think they might have found out about me though." She stops, looks up and smiles, then leans closer to the camera. "Staff on my floor have been walking cautiously past my desk for a few minutes. I think they're about to grab me. I'm going to make a run for it. Head to my mothers. Dixon, you'll remember where. Once this is all done, then you can come and meet me. I don't want to be there when it all goes down." She reaches for the camera and begins to walk off from her desk down the corridor towards the exit.

"Don't come looking for me before this is done. You'll only put yourselves at risk. They don't have any record of my mother's location, I won't use trackable transport. No doubt they'll get someone tracking you through the LAF database so if you leave the city to come to me, they'll follow you." She enters the lift to head to the main building entrance. "Good luck guys, I hope to god that I see you both again." She smiles a little. "Dixon, we may not be the same as we were, but know that I never stopped loving you". Her smile slips a little as her eyes start to water. The window then cuts out and folds back into the black box. Both Jimmy and Dixon lean back in their chairs. Jimmy looks to Dixon.

"Well, she's ok. We know that now"

Yet again emotions brim high as Dixon tries to contemplate this news. He'd always thought that Sadie had grown to despise him. Losing his daughters nearly killed him, and hearing her argue fiercely with him did nothing but pour salt on the wounds. After hearing her proclaim her true feelings, Dixon realised how wrong he'd been. He'd folded inwards into his own hate and depression. He too had never stopped loving her, he literally couldn't even if he tried. He sighs in relief, "yeah, so what do we do now, detective?" his face clearly more at ease. Jimmy stands up, collecting himself.

"We have the files, we're done with Chester. Time to go to Leistung." He says, turning to face Dixon.

"Who are we going to speak to?" Dixon asks. "We don't know anyone in their top levels. How do we get a sit down with them?"

Jimmy contemplates things for a few seconds, his face contorting as the gears in his head grind on. Finally, he breathes in, nodding to himself.

"Improvise!"

Chapter 18

The front of the Leistung corporate building is not guarded by fearsome looking professionals. Nor is it reaching for the sky in a vision of clean and perfect architecture. It stands, a tall building certainly, but looking similar to every other building around it. The only identifying feature is the large 'L' on its front. The inner corner at the bottom of the letter holding the rest of the company name.

Leistung hadn't poured resources into their assets outside of their territories. Setting up standard outposts throughout the globe simply to create an easier path of contact with their competitors. The bulk of their resources being recycled back into their South American empire. Only once they had bolstered their defences and technologies with their latest toys, would they begin rolling the previous generation of assets. The hand me down culture being laughed at on rival turf, Jimmy himself had been laughed at when he was a cop by Fenghuang goons, and even by a Leistung official carrying out a placement in his precinct.

The illusion of these outer footholds being inferior was exactly what Leistung had wanted. Not only did their competition become arrogant, but they didn't have any idea what the Leistung homeland was capable of. A case of keeping your enemies close but your guns closer.

Jimmy and Dixon strolled through the door of the building. The layout much like one would expect of an old business. A small seating area for people to sit and wait for their appointments. Three one hundred inch television screens, top of the range devices from nearly one hundred years ago. A gruff looking old man sitting behind a large wooden desk. A receptionist clearly too old to care who you wanted to see, and more interested in getting back to the TV show he'd put on the nearest television.

"Good day, old chap" Jimmy lays his hands on the reception countertop. The old man unblinking and unseeing, continues watching the TV. Jimmy tries again but still receives no reply.

Dixon looks to the TV also, the show a modern-day equivalent of the old family issues reality crap people used to watch when off work with nothing to do. Three women with long black hair and an ageing family likeness between them, spit volumes of Italian curses at a man smugly sitting in a chair. A chyron at the bottom rolls a message; "You left me for a cyber doll and now you want our sons to call her mom?!"

Dixon smiles, chuckling he turns to the desk. "Crazy bitches huh?" The old man grunts a single vowel reply. Dixon looks to Jimmy and continues. "This is the one where he isn't the dad of two of the kids and the last girl used to be a man." The old man's eyes wrinkle open as Dixon continues, "Yeah, he stole the dude's savings and got the bits switched".

"Hey! You just ruined that episode, you fuck!" his raspy voice bubbling with the spit of his frustration.

Dixon leans on the desk with folded arms. "Funny thing is, she still has a cock bigger than the dudes". Jimmy chuckles.

"I believe my friend was trying to ask you a question." Dixon nods in Jimmy's direction as the old man sits. Holding back further insults in his crinkles.

"We need to speak to one of the executives that are here, right now. I'm a LAF detective" He flashes his holo-badge. "It's of the utmost importance".

"That's all fine and dandy, sonny boy. But ain't nobody gets up to the execs unless <u>they</u> arrange it." His mouth almost hidden by the sagging skin around it, a tiny hole of black warping the words out. "Now I suggest you skedaddle, on your little feet out of here, and let me get back to my show". He looks to Dixon, "which you ruined".

Jimmy slaps the countertop, making the old man jump in surprise. Dixon even jolts unexpectedly. "Listen here, old timer, this shit is bigger than you or me or even the executives. We have to speak to the top fucking dog, or so help me I will beat another lifetime of pain into you." His jaw flexes as he stares the old man down.

"Gentlemen" a voice cuts through the situation from the side. Jimmy frowns as he looks across the room. A smartly dressed woman in a three-piece suit and waistcoat stands before them.

"It's alright, Jeeves. I'll talk to these guys." She turns back to Jimmy and Dixon, extending a hand. "Miss Maria Sorensen. It sounds like you have something of the utmost importance. How can I help you?"

Jimmy looks back at the old man as they walk over to greet the woman and shake her hand. The old man leans back in his chair, bouncing up quickly to shout "My name isn't Jeeves. It's Frank!"

"Thank you, Jeeves" Maria shouts back, as she leads the two men through double doors. Dixon walks behind Jimmy and Maria, an ogre in height and size by comparison.

"Thanks, Miss Sorensen. I'm Detective Kershon and this is my partner, Dixon Callaway." She looks up to Dixon. He smiles and adds, "Former partners" She lowers her eyebrows a little in confusion.

"We need to speak to one of your executives as soon as possible. We've got some information I think they're going to want to know about." Jimmy says.

"Oh, right this way, gentlemen." She leads them down the corridor and up two flights of stairs. Jimmy slows his pace a little and falls back in line with Dixon. Nudging him with his elbow and flashing his eyes at the woman's rear. Dixon sighs and looks back in disdain at his friend. Leaning into Jimmy's ear he whispers, "You gotta get a girl or get laid or something. Now focus!"

Jimmy nods and restores his professional manners. Miss Maria Sorensen looks to be in her mid-forties, not much shorter than Jimmy, her long blonde hair tied up with two chopsticks holding it in place. Two strands of her shining hair hang down, framing her face. Young and welcoming eyes pierce blue, her cheekbones and jawline giving her an attractive and strong appearance.

Opening a door to a small but respectable looking office she lets the two men enter. "Please take a seat," she says.

"Oh, are you going to get someone, it's really urgent we speak to someone now," Jimmy says, his voice beginning to show a little firmness. Maria smiles and circles the desk, sitting down behind it, quickly checking her screen.

"Right gentlemen, as I said I am Maria Sorensen and I am part of the Central America Leistung Legal team. You said you wanted an executive, well in this building I am about as close as you are going to get to that." Her eyes stabbing at Jimmy as his resolve dwindles away.

"Please, what is so urgent?" She looks to Dixon.

Jimmy leans forward again, "Uh, I'm sorry. I thought you were uh..."

"A receptionist? Please, let's not dabble on your misguided prejudices after you bring something urgent to me." She says, as Jimmy half smiles realising the humour of his own mistake. Apologising, he provides her with the information stored in his arm and explains the significance and consequences they feel may be on the horizon.

Dixon remains silent throughout the whole discussion. Knowing he wouldn't be able to add much to it, his mind wanders, hoping that Sadie made it to her mother's without a problem. Not knowing the lengths to which he would go to get revenge on anyone who hurt her. He had lost her once already, and now with the faint chance that he had of sharing love with her again, there was no chance even the largest army was going to get in his way.

"This is bizarre," Maria says as she gets the full picture painted to her by Jimmy, filling in the end of his sentences occasionally as her quick wit figures out pieces. Jimmy can't help but feel his heart flutter a little as he watches the lips of this beautiful woman talk in such an enchanting manner. Her words are more specific and professional than the terminology Jimmy can achieve. He watches, mesmerized as she rises from her desk.

"Gentlemen, thank you for this information. I have to get this to my superiors post haste. I'll be contacting all branches of Leistung legal, as well as Mr Engel." She pulls a notepad device from the screen and taps it a few times.

"Engel? Gabriel Engel?" Jimmy asks. Maria nods, smiling as she walks to the door. "Uh, Miss Sorensen, please take my contact details. We'd be very interested in providing any assistance to yourself and Mr Engel if need be." He swipes his arm and the pad in Maria's hand notifies her of his details.

"He will no doubt want to meet with you, good day gentlemen, and thank you". She nods to Dixon with a polite smile, and reaches out to shake Jimmy's hand. As she does so, she locks eyes with him and for a split second, it almost seems like she blushes.

Chapter 19

As they leave the building, Jimmy finally giving up trying to see where Maria had walked off to, they jump into the car and head off back towards Dixon's place.

"How does it feel?" Jimmy asks.

"How does what feel?" Dixon asks.

"Almost like we were back doing our old work together, huh?" Jimmy smiles, not speeding around traffic, his mood far more relaxed and at ease with himself.

"I'm not gonna lie, Kersh. It was feeling like that a bit" Dixon's eyes stay focussed straightforward. Jimmy hesitates.

"Was?"

"Yes, was. Until you laid your eyes on Sorensen back there. You never used to melt into a puddle" He smirks, a faint chuckle under his breath.

Jimmy nods as he leans an arm on the side of the car door. "Ok, yeah. Not my finest moment. I'm not gonna lie either, I like her". Dixon looks at him, ready to jab with another insult. He sees him looking at the road as he drives, but he can tell that he is interested in the woman. Not like he was with women back when they worked together. He didn't want to bed her, he could see that real spark in him. Mixed with the genuine feeling that he was doing some real police work, Jimmy looked the most comfortable he's ever been in his skin.

Looking back at the road, Dixon rests back into the seat. Closing his eyes he enjoys the feeling of almost being the motivated and strong-willed man he used to be years ago. He drifts off to sleep and wakes up as Jimmy pulls up to his apartment.

"Sorry, I must have drifted off," Dixon says, blinking his eyes clear.

"Not a problem, man. Figure that's some of the healthiest sleep you've had in a while." Jimmy says as Dixon exits the car. He leans over to talk out of the door.

"These guys are gonna make a move fast. Once word gets up to Engel, he'll want to question the council. I suspect we'll be called up pretty early tomorrow. I'll swing by and pick you up." Dixon nods in reply and closes the door. Returning upstairs to his apartment, he lets his mind rest as he eats a meal. Sitting down with a glass of whiskey, he swills it around after eating, thinking about what he'd achieved with Jimmy so far. Thinking about what he could achieve if everything turned out well. He could get back into an actual job again, maybe even join the force again. His biggest thought that after everything had gone down and he might be able to see Sadie again. Would she want to pick things up? Could they get married again? Would she want to start a new family?

With his eyes beginning to feel heavy, he tries to hold onto the last pieces of consciousness he has. Realising his vision has rested on his prosthetic arm, he gently closes his fingers.

Phantom feelings sting his comprehension almost as much as the silence that fills his home. There isn't a rattle from the empty bottle he holds in a shaky drunk hand, no numbness to hold back the truth that he'd lost RJ. She'd probably have had some mischievous wisecrack to throw at him right about now. "Back to the bottle?" or something like that. How could artificial intelligence feel so close to a friend, a loved one, another daughter?

Sniffling back the tears he wants to shed, he tries desperately to remind himself that she wasn't real. Simply a bunch of code some spotty geek had written in a crappy basement somewhere. He raises his forearm and runs his real fingers along the surface, it's so cold, so inhuman, yet all he can think about is the digital daughter he once had there. Now plastic and metal replaces it. Dropping his arm, he takes a deep breath and looking into nothing, drifts off.

Dixon wakes up, still in the chair, the empty whiskey glass still in his prosthetic hand. A series of bangs thunder from his door and he balls his fists quickly in reflex, the glass shattering, shards scattering across the room. Abruptly awake he opens the door. Jimmy stands on the other side, a nervous smile.

"I'm here, told you I'd pick you up" His smile lingering awkwardly.

"Why do you look weird?" Dixon asks.

"I didn't expect to get picked up myself," Jimmy says. Dixon frowns as he lets Jimmy enter. "So I got a call from Maria Sorensen asking for us to come in for a meeting. They think we'd be well placed to provide some footwork for them."

"Okay. That's good news right. Oh! Are you nervous about seeing her?" Dixon asks, changing his shirt.

"No, well, yeah. But when I was away to jump into my car to come get you, I got another call."

"Maria wanted to ask you out? Geez, she's got more balls than you. I think I like her too". Dixon fixes his collar.

"It wasn't Maria, it was Tom Sutcliffe, head of Halo," Jimmy says, Dixon halting suddenly, his collar still in his hands. "He'd heard that there was something going on with his legal team, and that there were Leistung execs suggesting Engel get in touch with him. Guess they must have some spies in the company or something".

"They all do" Jimmy finishes fixing his collar. "So Sutcliffe wants to see us too? Good. We can go see him after we see Engel."

"Not going to happen I'm afraid." Jimmy bows his head a little. "After he'd found out that we were the ones involved in this, uh...he had me picked up. There's a ride waiting outside waiting to take us to him."

Dixon stops as he exits the apartment, with Jimmy following close behind, he is both surprised and impressed. "He works fast, huh? I like that" he continues on down the stairs and out of his building. A large shuttle sits at the kerbside, a stunning looking piece of technology that was drawing lots of attention. The Halo logo across the back half of it in a sleek design. A man stands at the door, a smart suit, expensive haircut and expressionless face all scream that he is security.

Walking up to the vehicle, the man steps aside, with a vague gesture to enter the vehicle. Dixon looks down at the man, assessing whether he was being forced or assisted. The man looks up at him and in a flat tone says "Good day, Mr Callaway. Please enter the shuttle and we'll have you at Halo momentarily". The robotic tone of their employees is a little haunting.

They climb into the shuttle and take a seat. The luxury and comfort is obvious upon sitting down. The interior doing its best not to show off any specific feature, but also screaming that it is better than anything you will ever see in your life. The man sits down facing Jimmy and Dixon, and speaks to the driver in the front briefly. The shuttle doors bolt closed with a reassuring clunk, and Jimmy looks out the window as they ascend out of the neighbourhood, watching the people gawk at the shuttle as it picks up speed, flying through the air like it was rolling on a smooth roller coaster.

Dixon looks out through the front window of the shuttle as they continue to fly higher and higher, noticing that they are not joining the streams of flying vehicles working their way between the buildings. Ascending above them still, he sees the clouds that hide the tops of the most important structures. Pushing into the cloud the sky goes dark. Looking through the front window the clouds prevent any real view. The heads-up display highlights the outline of buildings as they rise and finally burst through the clouds.

Light fills the cabin again, blinding Dixon and Jimmy's. They squint as the shuttle begins to level off. Looking around they now see a white fluffy floor with only a few towers stretching above it.

"It's like heaven or something," Jimmy says to Dixon. The guard cracks a faint smile at the gentlemens' amazement.

"If you could buy your way past the pearly gates" Dixon adds, his comment causing the guard to look down his nose at him. The shuttle pulls up to the largest of the towers. A landing dock juts out of the side near the very top of the building, it's spire reaching higher still. As the landing feet of the shuttle unfold from the body, and it gently takes its place on the dock, the guard stands. Exiting the vehicle and holding the door open, he turns.

"This way, gentlemen" his eyes fix on Dixon's and a fake smile appears on his face. Jimmy exits first, followed by Dixon who hunches over to get out. The entire top of the building is plated with thick dark glass. Only the faint shadow of the inside can be seen - another three floors are visible. A few people mingle around on the current level, three figures appear to be on the second floor and the top floor is empty.

The guard leads the way inside. Two shining black doors, eight feet in width, slide apart with sharply. Dixon spots a bar as the centrepiece of the room. A man wearing a monocle stands behind the bar, a white shirt with a checked waistcoat and a white light shooting up from inside his collar. As he smiles, waving to them, his teeth appear to glow with light. Noticing the large curling hair style, purple in colour, Dixon then realises that almost everyone on this floor is decked out in similar flamboyant outfits. They sit around chatting, with snooty poses, sipping from extravagant looking cocktails in even more glamorous looking vials. Their conversation difficult to distinguish, even Jimmy struggles to pick out the words due to the put on posh tones and dialect.

The guard continues on to a staircase, looking back he sees that both Dixon and Jimmy are standing awestruck in the middle of the room.

"Gentlemen, a drink perhaps?" the bartender asks. Dixon is about to turn and ask for something as the rest of the room goes quiet, like an old western, they all look at the two drably dressed men before them.

"How did this filth get in here?" one particularly pretentious looking woman says, breaking the silence. "This place isn't for low-level GIDs like you. Away peasant" her lips curling almost as much as her nose as she turns back to her drink, looking for the adoration of her peers.

"They are with me." A voice with a strong Australian twang echoes out from above. Looking up, the room sees a tall man leaning on a rail, overlooking the entire bar area. The previously snobbish woman now holds her tongue and looks extremely embarrassed.

The Australian walk around to the stairs and shouts "Come on, guys. Up here!" He beckons for Dixon and Jimmy to join him. As they walk up the stairs, Dixon receives another counterfeit smile from the guard.

"I see you've made friends with Bob" the Australian chortles as they reach the top of the stairs. He throws his arms around Jimmy, patting his back warmly. Looking up at Dixon he laughs again.

"Holy shit stacks, you're nearly taller than this building." He extends his hand and feigns pain as Dixon shakes it. "Please, let's have a seat" He gestures to the room he came from, two figures are sitting in the room. He opens the door and gives them a quick gesture.

"Off you fuck!" he says, and they do.

Jimmy manages to catch his breath, "Are you Tom Sutcliffe?"

"In the flesh. The one and only. Head of Halo, and most famous of the rich philanthropists on this fine planet". Both men look back at him blankly. He coughs and corrects his stance. "Uh, yes. Tom Sutcliffe, at your service".

Chapter 20

Tom Sutcliffe was not what they expected. He was known for being a big character, but also as a brutally intelligent and professional businessman. His commercials and news interviews had shone a very positive light on him. Almost everyone who saw him liked him within seconds. Not because of his handsome face and strong jawline. Nor due to his entertaining outfits, which although giving the appearance of suited and booted CEO, were also decadent and bright.

Neither Dixon nor Jimmy would have thought that the man who essentially ran the entirety of North America would be such a friendly person.

"You two are both cops, right?" he asks, hesitating. "Well, you are, you used to be" he points to Dixon as he circles the large glass table in the centre of the room. He claps his hands twice and the wall unfolds presenting another private bar. Picking up a large dispenser containing a very dark spirit he turns.

"Single or double?" Tom asks as Dixon pulls up a seat at the far end of the table.

"Single for me," Jimmy says.

"Make it a triple" Dixon says smiling, shrugging to Jimmy as Tom turns back to three glasses already lined up on the bar top. Pouring the drinks he takes two over to the table, looking up and flashing his smile again, he pushes the glasses, sliding them across the full length of the table. The rolling sound of the glasses bouncing around the room before cutting as Jimmy and Dixon catch their drinks.

Lifting his own drink Tom toasts. "To the police and all the sacrifices they make for everyone else's safety". He throws back the double he'd poured and swallows it in one. Dixon and Jimmy sip theirs, both feeling the sharp bite of a very well-aged rum. Tom walks up to the seat next to Jimmy and sits on the table instead.

"Now, gentlemen. I'm sure you've been made aware of my request to speak to you. I don't mean to be rude or ruin your day, but I've been quite disturbed at the stories I've been hearing surrounding you two." He squeezes his eyebrows together, looking as serious as possible.

Jimmy is about to explain as Tom cuts him off. "You can imagine my surprise when I hear that several files have been stolen and sent to LAF authorities by one of my legal team's receptionists." He points across the table at Dixon. "You're ex-wife, no?"

"Uh - yes," Dixon flutters.

"Indeed, then I'm told that you have been rustling up a meeting with the big wigs at Leistung. Something about an inside scoop on us that'll give them the advantage." He leans closer to Jimmy a little, "correct?"

"Mr Sutcliffe, first of all, let me thank you for having us up here. I don't think either of us would have ever dreamed of seeing something like this" he looks at Dixon who shakes his head with an upturned lip. "The fact is that we found an actual paper copy of a legal document in a Fenghuang employee's apartment."

"Fenghuang?" Tom's features scrunch. "Filthy scum have been trying to set up a base in Denver. Trying to train spies up to infiltrate my business, Leistung too for that matter. What did the file say?"

"It was a legal document outlining the merger of Fenghuang and Halo," Dixon says. He swigs his rum and looks back at Tom with a firm glance.

"A merger? Why would we- oh! Those sneaky shits. They are probably specking up documents to put behind fake new employees to send into Halo HQ. They tried this about fifteen years ago. Caught three of them and another killed herself jumping off the one hundred and fourth floor."

"So you have no plans to merge with them?" asks Jimmy.

"On the contrary, those two I just kicked out are part of my legal team. We're setting up to try and push them further out of Colorado and Kansas. I was actually going to be hiring up some Leistung muscle" He taps Jimmy on the shoulder. "Maybe I should keep you guys in mind. Brains go well with brawn."

"My ex-wife. She said that she was being tracked by you guys. That true?" Dixon's voice low and pointed.

"Well of course. We aren't seeking a merger with one of our main competitors, but if our internal staff are shipping off important documents to external sources without our permission - we tend to pay close attention to that sort of thing." Tom jokes. "I can reassure you, she would come to no harm if we found her. The worst case scenario - she would be questioned on her motives and given a severance package.

Maybe not the best package but she wouldn't leave empty-handed."

Dixon asks "Do you have any idea where she went?"

"Last we heard she'd fled the city. Somebody went to her home address but didn't find her. Apparently, someone else had been looking for her. A few bodies turned up there." Tom's eyes get more serious "after we found out that, we knew things weren't just as simple as someone selling our contracts for a quick buck".

He stands from the table, pulling the chair out and sitting down, putting his feet up. "A friendly source at Leistung, one Maria Sorensen informed us of the details you had passed on to her. She just so happens to be heading up the recruitment process there for our hired protection. Gave us the news as a show of good faith."

"Did she mention me at all?" Jimmy asks in as his concentration wanders.

"You? She mentioned your names" Tom says. "What? You got a thing for this girl or something?"

"Or something..." Dixon says, the other two turning to look at him like he'd just insulted their mothers. "Mr Sutcliffe, the document didn't only mention a merger. There was a framework for altering the GID hierarchy. Lows and mids would be one new low level. High's an execs would be a new High, and you council members would remain at the top."

"Why change the GIDs?" Tom asks rhetorically, standing and walking around to lean at the end of the table. "They want to simplify the GIDs to create a large slave base?" He asks, looking up. Dixon and Jimmy nod back at him. "This goes against what the council have been seeking for years. We've been trying to find common ground to bring everyone forward, raise everyone's standard of life." He thinks further. "Hell, I'd just been working on some plans with Esther Beneventi of Praetorium"

"Is it possible that this file may have been the beginning of Fenghuang infiltrating your company and looking to take over? If they did, putting through this GID change would be far easier." Jimmy says, "They'd be able to strong-arm the other council members into agreeing."

"Yes, you're right. This has to be stopped" Tom stands up and taps his temple. A circle of metal glimmers and then unfolds a series of short arms that curve around his ear and down his cheek. "Gentlemen, I need to speak to the other council members. Please take the shuttle to wherever you want, be ready for us to contact you at any time." He walks to the door and signals them to leave.

As Jimmy and Dixon exit, the doors close and Tom's voice can be heard very sternly shouting for someone to get him Leistung and Praetorium as soon as possible. The guard approaches them with a far friendlier expression.

"Gentlemen, I've been informed to give you a ride to wherever you choose. Where do you want to go?" he asks politely.

"Dix, where to?" Jimmy asks. The guard looks up, almost apologetic for his previous demeanour.

"That shuttle got tracking?" asks Dixon.

"The only person with clearance to track it is Mr Sutcliffe himself." The guard states.

"Perfect, let's take it to Sadie's mother's," Dixon says to Jimmy. "Fenghuang won't track the shuttle, and even if they do they won't want to cause a mess of Tom Sutcliffe's shuttle".

"Could be risky - but ok," Jimmy says after thinking it over. The three men turn to the stairs, walking down, a few of the colourful guests notice them. Looking down and holding their silence, they watch as Jimmy and Dixon exit the bar area. Whispering to each other about who they might be, and trying to figure out why Tom Sutcliffe wanted to speak to them.

Getting into the shuttle, Dixon informs the driver of their destination. Nodding from behind the black helmet attached to the ceiling of the shuttle he turns back, gripping the throttle and pushing it forward, the noise of the propulsion rumbles as they take off. The shuttle soars over the clouds for several miles. Jimmy looks out the windows at the endless waves of clouds. Feeling almost like they were flying off to the end of a story, he admires the beauty.

After a few minutes, the shuttle begins to descend. Piercing into the cloud floor once again, the cabin goes dark, emerging through the clouds and back into the grimmer daylight of the lower level. Rain pouring down on the city as if Poseidon wanted to wash it away, the drops of water batter the shuttle and almost deafens its's passengers.

As they descend closer to buildings the lights reflect off the droplets, making it harder to distinguish objects. Blues, purples, greens and reds bounce around almost like a disco. Dixon looks into the cockpit, the driver appears unfazed. The helmet no doubt using a built-in scanner and projector to display a HUD with everything clear as day. The drivers head switches right quickly looking at something in the distance. He alters the course of the shuttle and a light beeping can be heard from the cockpit, the rain almost drowning it out. Dixon listens closely, the beeping sound closer to a warning than anything else.

The driver slaps at something in the cockpit and the lights in the cabin fade darker, all three of them turning a dark red.

"Gentlemen, please harness yourself in," the guard says, as he pulls the arm straps off his own seat and clips himself in.

"What's going on?" Jimmy asks, as he manages to fumble his arms through the harness.

"I'm sure it's just the bad weather. Don't worry, this pilot's an ace." says the guard, his tone confident.

As Dixon clips the buckle on his harness, he sees the pilot look off to the right again, slamming at the control wheel. The shuttle quickly spins, completing a full aileron roll, bright light fills the cabin for a second and shoots on past them. Dixon and Jimmy try to gather their bearings from suddenly being thrust upside down. The guards face no longer looks back reassuringly, but now shows concern as he looks out of the windows, trying to trace the light.

"Missile!" The pilot shouts back as he begins evasive manoeuvres. The shuttle ducks lower between the buildings as several sharp bursts of light shoot past. Looking out the back window, Dixon sees the pulse rounds firing furiously from the front of a black slim line. As the gunfire stops and both shuttles sharply turn amongst buildings, the outline of the rival becomes clearer.

A matte black vessel looking almost as flat as a stingray, save for the wing tips which split out. Two large mini-guns churn out more rounds in their direction, as the targeting system tries to get a lock for the barrage of missiles waiting to be loosed on either side of the cockpit. The pilot cannot be seen due to the tinting of the windshield. A thin red line peaks the tip of the shuttle, almost a sinister grin of light.

The gunfire from the black enemy pierces through several buildings, and as both shuttles edge lower and lower, the wake of their flightpaths drag up garbage from the street. Dust and dirt speed along like fog chasing the two vehicles.

"Hold on!" the pilot shouts as he yanks back on the wheel. The shuttle quickly begins to ascend at a sharp angle. As he does so, he curves the shuttle around an apartment block. People run to their windows as they pass, shaking the windows.

As they reach the apex of the building, the pilot quickly cuts the engines and slams on the air brake and rudders, flipping the shuttle to point straight down to the earth. In the view downwards, the black shuttle can be seen circling the structure as it ascends, unable to fly up as quickly, but able to corner far more sharply. As gravity wraps its hand around the Halo shuttle, the pilot smashes the engines back to full power. Jimmy and Dixon try to hold onto their inner organs as they violently descend.

The pilot spins the shuttle counterclockwise around the building, in a conflicting path to the black shuttle flight pattern. On opposite sides, the circle closer and closer, until finally, the Halo shuttle descends below the black one. Pulling out the pilot fires off over the city top.

"Think we'll be alright now" the pilot looks back, giving a thumbs up, the guard breathing a little easier in the chair.

"Who was that?" Jimmy asks.

"Best bet? A Fenghuang ship. They occasionally try and pick off some of our delivery ships, and blame gangs and hijackers for it. They've never come after this ship before though. ID tags should make them know better" the guard says.

Dixon looks out of the back window as the rain and refracting light consumes the cabin again. The engine trail of the black shuttle still ascends the building. Just as he is about to turn around and unbuckle to relax, he notices the red tip of the shuttle go out. Nearly two thirds up the building, the shuttle also cuts its engines, almost instantaneously turning to face away from the building and in their direction.

A ball of light shines from the building as the engines kick back in, and the shuttle almost kicks off the building. Windows shatter and the holes left in their place singe like freshly burned paper.

"We're not done yet" Dixon shouts to the pilot. Before he can finish repeating to the questioning pilot, a plethora of phosphorous lights spread out of the black shuttle and begin quickly gaining ground on them.

"Missile barrage incoming!" the guard shouts, peering out the back. Again the pilot attempts to roll his way deeper towards the city buildings. This time missiles close in on either side, above and below. Edging closer and boxing in the shuttle one missile cuts closer and explodes about five feet away. The pilot adjusts as best he can, but can't pull the shuttle out of a sudden dive. Further missiles cut in to take a stab, exploding around the shuttle as they nearly skim off a building top. The shuttle shakes violently as the explosions vibrate through the chassis. Instruments in the cockpit flicker, some turn off entirely. Bolts and welded seals begin to clatter, as the shuttle struggles to hold itself together. The pilot then screams in fear.

"Brace for impact" The final missile in chase hits with one of the rear engines, launching the shuttle into a corkscrew. It smashes through the corner of a large office building and falls like a poorly thrown stone.

Chapter 21

Smashing through the roof of another building, the shuttle had come to a rest in a wrecked heap in the middle of a production factory. Dixon and Jimmy hang from their harnesses as the Shuttle faces nose downwards into a series of robotic machines. The other parts of the factory still churn away, oblivious to the huge hole in the roof and demolished production line.

Dixon's eyes lightly flicker open. A view of a crumpled cabin before him, the guard still in his seat, buckled in tightly. He no longer looks like a robot impersonating a human, the crash bending the chassis that held his seat in place. A few seconds pass before Dixon realises that the guard's neck has moved around seven inches to the left, and his hips and limbs sit at a most inhuman angle. Small droplets of blood drip from his mouth and a couple of cuts elsewhere.

The shock kicks in, and Dixon recalls what had happened moments earlier. Blinking he looks across to Jimmy, still unconscious, but certainly still pieced together correctly. A couple of small cuts mark his face from the glass that must have shattered in the back window. Pulling his dangling arms up, Dixon releases himself from the harness.

Nearly landing on top of the guard, he sees just how bad the man's body was broken. There was no way that this man could have been a robot, not with the remnants of human organs Dixon could now see inside the poor soul.

Unfortunately, the manufacturing lines production of metal rods, used for adding strength to walls had skewered through the pilot and held him in a terrifying pose. His arms up covering his face, clearly, he knew the inevitability of his fate. The rods poke through the back of the pilot and glimmer clean. The lower portions of the rods grow a dark scarlet as blood runs down them. Dixon turns back to Jimmy.

"Hey buddy, come on, wake up," he says, combatting the dizzy feeling in his head, while lightly slapping Jimmy's face. No response.

"You ain't dying on me, ugly" he slaps Jimmy harder, his head jolting in reply but still nothing. Dixon places two fingers on his neck and finds a pulse, taking a sigh of relief, he unbuckles Jimmy.

"Nearly had me there" Jimmy's body slumps onto Dixon's shoulder, as he then reaches for the manual release on the door. Turning the handle upwards the door ejects off the side of the shuttle and clatters into the back of the factory. Dixon gets his footing set to climb out of the shuttle with Jimmy as he is blinded by light once again. This time the light brings him a little out of the shock that had set into him. Pain thunders through his head like a sledgehammer and he squints to look up.

"Well hello there gorgeous," a voice says, before several arms pull Jimmy free from Dixon's grip. Dixon shields his eyes from the light before more arms wrap around him and pull him free from the wreckage. Still being blinded he asks, "You've got to help us, we just got attacked" his panic falls on deaf ears and he is shoved off of the manufacturing line.

Several boots can be heard moving around him as a silhouetted figure approaches him.

"We are here to help" a calm viperous voice whispers in his ear, and is sharply followed be a brutal club to the back of his head. Darkness.

Chapter 22

Water splashes on Dixon's face, a cheap trick to wake someone from being knocked unconscious. The difference is that unlike the movies people don't spring to life again after this. Dixon slowly emerges from his slumber, the cold and damp of the water slightly soothing to the rest of the feelings he grows aware of.

"Look alive, big guy," a voice says to him, slightly familiar. Dixon recalls it as the voice that spoke to him before he was knocked out. Raising his head and looking around his arms feel tired and sore, both of them tied above his head with tight nylon straps and metal buckles. His joints ache and muscles swarm with waves of agony, the result of having been in a crash then assaulted and carelessly moved to an unknown location. His jacket discarded and his shirt removed, his bare chest heaving in the cold of the room, steam rises from his skin.

Looking up Dixon see the person talking to him, as he tries to stop himself from falling unconscious again. A short man stands with his arms behind his back. Dixon on his knees - the man stands just at eye level with him, smiling. A dark armour surrounds his body, masking his physique a little. Dixon surmises that if someone wears armour like that, and meets people in this fashion he is probably someone to watch out for.

The armour appears almost like a series of shimmering black pads stuck to a second skin suit. The second skin looking almost carbon fibre like and the pads backlit with a yellow hue.

"You're a nosey one, Mr Callaway," the man says "should have learned to stay out of things when you retired. Now we're going to need to extract as much information as possible before you breathe your last insignificant puff." He steps closer to Dixon, a picture of David and Goliath, if David had been a sadistic hunter who liked to toy with his prey. Parting his hands from behind his back, he shows that he is holding a plasma baton with two hooks at the top end of it, sharp metal surging with power.

"If you give me what then you won't have to get acquainted with my tools." The man inspects the baton, the red light illuminating his face like a child holds a torch to their face, when they tell ghost stories. "Fail to provide me with what I want, and this is only the first tool you'll get to know intimately. It's going to be fun breaking you, I'm sure your friend will enjoy the screams he hears from the next room."

"Fuck you," Dixon says, spitting at the man, sweat pouring down his chest. The short man smiles again and props Dixon's head up with the baton, the energy pulsing into his chin not expelling the full charge. Whipping the baton back the man spins around with martial art precision. The baton sharply collides with Dixon's right side, digging into his ribs.

Dixon screams in pain, the plasma singeing his flesh and coursing through his muscles, as the bladed hook digs in and scrapes at the bone.

"Where were you headed in the Halo shuttle?" The man asks.

"Your mother's," Dixon says, while gritting his teeth. The baton turns and widens the wound sending more pain through his abdomen.

"Where?" The man asks again. Dixon breathes heavily, mustering the strength to hurl another insult. "I bet you were heading off to rescue that pretty ex-wife of yours."

"You leave Sadie alone!" Dixon looks into the man's eyes. The mention of Sadie sending adrenaline coursing through his body, instantly the pain subsides. "I'll tear you apart if you touch her."

"I look forward to it. What did you talk to Tom Sutcliffe about?" the man asks another question.

"Tom? He just came from your mother's" Dixon manages to push a sharp chuckle through the pain. The baton swiftly exits the small hole and swings round in a flurry. Colliding with the other side the man throws a kick into the original wound. His foot may be one of the smallest Dixon has ever taken, but the force and technique used almost shatter his entire rib cage.

"Your buddy is getting questioned next door you know. You think he's going to try and put on this brave act as well?" the man says leaning in. Dixon smells the unsubtle aftershave he's caked himself in.

"Jimmy isn't going to tell you shit, just like I won't. Nice to know you want to hear about Tom Sutcliffe though. He's going to want to shove that toy up your ass after he finds out you killed his personal guard and wrecked his ride." Dixon smiles, receiving a punch for his troubles, his lip bursting instantly.

"Tom might get pissed with us, but he isn't going to stop us chopping you up and feeding you both piece by piece to the rats in Chinatown," The man says pulling the baton from Dixon's ribs and stepping back, curling down in a martial arts pose the man breathes in heavily.

"Now, how did you find out that Chester Lopez was in possession of the dossier?"

With blood lining the bottom row of his teeth, Dixon flashes a disgusting smile. "I told you already, your mother told us". He coughs a little of the blood as he laughs. His stomach tightening up as it cringes and aches.

The man spins the baton around himself quickly and cartwheels towards Dixon, shooting into the air in a large arching flip, the baton glimmering into focus as it swings down.

"Yanluo!"

The man halts the baton's bladed tip just next to Dixon's neck. The warmth of the plasma boiling the sweat on his skin. The man's head turns to the entrance of the dark room. Nothing is present in the room, barely any light aside from the spotlight on Dixon. Matte black tiles lead to the door in formation, where the silhouette of a female figure stands.

"That's enough!" the voice of the woman commands sharply. The man, Yanluo, steps back and faces the woman as she begins to approach, stopping next to him. He bows and departs to the side of the room. Tapping a tile, a chunk of the wall bevels outwards and slides open, a selection of close quarters combat weapons hang from the revealed cabinet. Knives, scythes, hammers, oddly shaped bladed weapons, presumably used for specific levels of torture. He turns off the plasma and wipes the bladed end on his glove before placing it in an empty slot on the wall. Turning back he leans against the wall with one foot bent onto it, watching Dixon intently from afar.

"Mr Callaway, I'm glad I can meet with you face to face. I always find a more personal interaction carries weight." The woman says, still drenched in darkness. Her accent tinted with a faint Chinese discipline.

"And you are?" Dixon asks, his strong build hulking before her. She takes two steps forward into the light, black stilettos emerge from the darkness and thin legs follow.

"My name is Myra Yang," she says as the rest of her body is revealed. A black Chinese dress lined with red frames her leg and waist. Red flowers swirl around a bird that ascends the left side of the dress. The eye on the bird, a ruby that shines, once in the light. Her hair tied up in a graceful knot at the top of her head allowing one curtain to drop down her back. She must be in her mid to late forties. Dixon notices she doesn't have two chopsticks holding her hair in place, but two miniature dao swords.

"I am the CEO of Fenghuang" Her dark red lipstick parting for her snake tongue to almost flicker as she talks. Her eyes appear to drip red as she peers into Dixon's face and character.

"You came all the way down here to speak to me? I guess I should be grateful" Dixon says.

"Oh, Mr Dixon, please. We here at Fenghuang have always prided ourselves on our meticulous attention to the finer details in life. I myself take a great interest as to why people do what they do. It gives you a better understanding of those around you" she leans forward slightly, "and how to exploit them." She turns and circles around him, her leg edging out of the slit in her dress. Dixon watches her stalk around him.

"I bet that you are also wondering why we are doing what we are doing. It's quite simple really, control." She slithers around to the other side quickly, catching Dixon in surprise as she talks into his ear. "Control over the situations around us allows us to dictate how we would like them to result. Like a bookie having a tip that a boxer will lose a match at a certain round. Having full knowledge of your intentions gives us that advantages."

She returns to the front of him. "I suppose you want to understand why we had that merger put in place though? Truth is, there was never a scheme to try and infiltrate Halo. It wasn't even our idea, to begin with."

"What? Who the hell was it then?" Dixon asks confused.

"That would be where I come in" A familiar voice echoes.

Chapter 23

The voice cutting into Dixon's attention, he notices a figure shadowing behind Myra Yang. Had he been there the whole time?

"You see, I've wanted to bring the world together ever since day one" the accent confirms Dixon's surprise as Tom Sutcliffe steps into the light. Dressed head to toe in black; shoes, suit, tie, even his eyes seem to be soulless.

Dixon struggles in his bindings, "You motherfucker!" - managing to push himself up enough to swing a foot at him.

"Now Dixon. There's no need to get angry. This is all for the greater good. You and your friend, unfortunately, stepped into the middle of everything and made a big old mess." Tom bows slightly to Myra, she returns the gesture of gratitude.

"So you were involved all along?" Dixon spits.

"Of course" he spreads his arms smiling. "This is all my brainchild, the future of our planet. Just think, with this merger we'll have no problem bending the rest of the council to our will". He looks into Myra's eyes almost flirtatiously. The thought of more power exciting both of them.

"The only real question I had, when I thought of it, was who to partner with. There's no way Leistung, Coracle or Praetorium would want to team up with me. None of them have the cunning I needed, Fenghuang on the other hand, well, we all know how brutally efficient they can be." He kneels down and flashes an eager grin, eyes wide.

"Imagine how thrilled I was when Lady Yang returned our interest. The two of us running the entire globe! Oh, and let's not forget the reconfiguring of our GID system. All of that new potential workforce, we'd be able to throw up buildings and tear down others like that." He clicks his fingers.

"You want to force half the world into slavery, you really think everyone will sit down and take it?" Says Dixon.

"You have this the wrong way, Mr Dixon" Lady Yang pipes up. "With the merging of Fenghuang and Halo the technological power and the disciplined numbers would mean that we can employ the most efficient means to bring us all to a better future. All of the problems the poor and low-level GIDs have, would quickly become a thing of the past. We could live in a world where nobody needs to worry about getting their next month's rent, or paying for the power."

Dixon stretches his back. "Sounds like you're already well prepped for the advertising campaign."

Tom rests his hand on Lady Yang's shoulder. "There are only a few small details we need to take care of."

"So you kill Jimmy and me. Then what?" asks Dixon.

"Oh, aren't you forgetting someone?" Tom boasts. Chortling under his breath, Yanluo returns pushing someone wearing a hood, their hands bound behind their back. Yanluo kicks the back of their knees, the figure falls to the ground, and a faint yelp pushes through the gag underneath the hood.

"How could you forget?" Tom asks sadistically, whipping the hood off. Sadie's eyes squint, taking in the light before whimpering at the sight of Dixon.

"Sadie?" Dixon gasps, tripping over his breath as he checks her up and down. Her hair a mess from an obvious struggle, her makeup trailing tear lines down her face. Dried blood clings to her nose and chin.

Tom joyfully watches Dixon squirm. "You really think that we'd let her get away. Oh, by the way, we found her about two minutes after she sent you that little love letter." He steps around and rests his hand on top of Sadie's head. "We ensure that we have tracking devices on all of our employees." He leans into Sadie's face, "Didn't tell you that, did we? Sorry" He smirks.

"You monster, let her go" Dixon screams, his eyes fixed on Sadie's.

"Sorry, big guy, can't be letting her run around stirring up trouble. She'd end up bringing back all her exes just to get the media ranting about our plans". Yanluo pulls a curved blade from a sheath in his back, and hands it to Tom. "People might not like it to start with, but they'll come round eventually. They'll write our names in history, and forever more we'll be remembered as the heroes of our era." He lowers the inner edge of the blade around Sadie's neck. Her face quivering with fear, further tears spill from her bloodshot eyes.

"Don't hurt her". Dixon's tone changes from his usual gritty sandpaper gruffness, to a lighter sympathetic appeal. "Don't hurt her, Tom." In reply, Tom smiles and lightly turns the blade a little. Sadie cries through her gag, in pain as a thin line of blood trails her neck.

"It's unfortunate, she really is a pretty one, Dixon. Alas, with any step forward for mankind, there have to be a few sacrifices." Tom says, pulling the blade through Sadie's neck in one swift motion.

Sadie stares at Dixon in pure shock. She can hear nothing at all, only seeing her ex-husband kneeling restrained in front of her, his mouth wide as he screams with everything in his lungs. She doesn't hear the ferocity of his pain. She sees his eyes fill with tears as he thrashes. Lowering her head slightly, she sees the river of red running down her front. She feels tired, and a calming warmth beginning to work its way up her legs, her fingertips resting, and her eyes getting heavy. Dixon continues to struggle, screaming loudly with every breath he sucks in. She looks up slowly as her ears begin to function again.

"Sadie, Sadie, no." Dixon's screams turning to compassion as their eyes lock again. Sadie's lips move, her jaw opens slightly but only a faint breeze of breath leaves her mouth. Dixon can still make out her mouthing of the words "I love you". He stops struggling and looks back defeated.

"Sadie, I always loved you, I've never stopped." He watches as the colour disappears from her face, her eyes roll back a little and her head drops. She slumps forward a little before her body falls to the side, blood still pouring from the gash in her neck. Tom looks at the edge of the blade, stained with blood, watching droplets fall from the tip. He inhales sharply and hands the blade back to Yanluo, who wipes it clean on his leg then sheathes it.

"I don't take pride in doing these things," Tom says, talking to Dixon's slouched body. "Maybe we could have been friends if things were different. Lady Yang here is a fierce drinker, you two would probably have a great time over a bottle". He watches as the sweat drips off Dixon, his silence piercing the room for several moments.

"How could we be friends?" his voice reverberating from his stomach. "I'm a low-level GID, right?" He raises his head slowly. "Council fucks like you don't socialise with the help, do you?" his eyes still watering, his face no longer cowering in terror and sadness, his cheeks, eyes and grin almost flex as he peers back at Tom.

Lady Yang laughs, "He's not wrong, Tom. I don't associate with lesser beings". Tom smirks and nods.

"Lesser beings? Like an animal? The worst thing to do with an animal is trying to take everything from it." Dixon says, growling as he manages to push his legs from the ground. His arms burning already, they throb, ready to burst as he pulls himself up. All three facing him step back a little as they see the giant rise.

Tom gathers composure, "We haven't taken everything yet. There's still your buddy. Then you!" He steps closer, showing dominance in front of his peers. Dixon quickly pulls at his binding with his prosthetic arm, swinging himself, his trunk-like leg crosses paths with Tom's head. A boot smothering his face and knocking him three feet back to the ground. Tom just manages to hold consciousness, wiping his mouth of blood, then gesturing to Lady Yang's enforcer.

Dixon plants his feet as Yanluo cautiously steps forward, reaches behind his back again and pulls out the curved blade, pulling a second similar blade in his other hand. He swings the blades around before jumping towards Dixon. In a display of practised technique, he nicks Dixon's calf. Unfortunately, he hadn't taken account of his targets sudden lack of interest in his own survival. Dixon, having witnessed the loss of his ex-wife threw his legs at Yanluo not caring if he lost one entirely. He only needed to plant one foot, the rest would sort itself out. In his feral rage, he manages to tussle both legs around Yanluo's head. Clenching tight, he almost cuts off his enemy's breath. Yanluo grabs at Dixon's legs as he struggles to catch air, one arm stretched up trying to swipe the blade at Dixon's face.

"Fuck!" Tom says, as Dixon locks eyes on him, watching the fear as he sharply twists his legs in opposing paths, a vicious snap rings through the room. Lady Yang jumps in disgust. Dixon quickly bites at the blade in Yanluo's hand before it goes limp. Gripping it in his teeth, he drops the body. The thump of Yanluo's body and the clang of the second blade send Tom and Lady Yang back a few steps.

Dixon yanks himself up to his bindings, first managing to cut the strap around his new arm, grabbing the blade in his hand and then releasing the second. He falls to the ground, partially landing on Yanluo with one knee. His weight crushing the body as Dixon's vision locks on the two people edging away from him. He rolls his shoulders, hearing the crack as they return to comfort, and leak away lactic acids. Leaning down, he grabs the blades and stands in the spotlight again. Steam rising from his hulking body, he begins to walk towards Lady Yang and Tom. A smile growing on his face.

Tom squeals in panic, pushing Lady Yang as he turns and bolts for the door. Lady yang stumbles forwards towards Dixon screaming. Her scream cuts short as Dixon catches his chin with the miniature scythes, piercing through the bottom of her chin and pointing out of her mouth. Through mumbled panic, she begs for mercy. Dixon's bear-like growling shout nearly bursts her eardrums as he yanks the blade from her mouth. Her jaw splits, firing blood and saliva up as her tongue flops. Dixon spins round bringing the other blade up and jamming it at her head. Yanluo clearly kept on top of sharpening the blade, as Lady

Yang's head jumps three inches from her shoulders and rolls off the back, her body following her head to the ground. Dixon exhales great gasps of angry grunts. He looks at Sadie's body, a pool of red surrounds her like a velvet cushion.

Dropping the blades he runs over and picks up her head, resting it on his knee. Her eyes and mouth are open, no semblance of life can be seen on her face though. Dixon weeps as he holds his forehead to hers, eyes closed. The woman who he'd loved had been taken from him. His children had been taken from him. He kisses her lightly on the forehead and closes her eyes. Laying her back down softly, Dixon's mind clears a little.

"Jimmy!" He realises.

Chapter 24

Bursting through the door to Jimmy's room Dixon sees a man standing at the side, dressed similarly to Yanluo, and also looking at a collection of blades and weapons on a secret cabinet on the wall.

"Dixon," Jimmy asks, looking across from his restraints and spotlight, the silhouette of his friend rising and falling with his growling breaths. The guard turns, his eyes panicking as he sees the brute in the doorway now approaching him. He grabs two hook swords from the wall and stretches his arms out, awaiting Dixon.

Dixon halts gripping the blades tight, locking eyes with the guard he throws one in Jimmy's direction, it slices through the binding, freeing his right arm. The blade clatters to the ground and Jimmy swiftly grabs it to free his other arm. Joining Dixon's side, the two eye up the guard.

"What took you so long?" Jimmy says. Dixon says nothing but charges. Jimmy does his best to follow close behind, but reaches the fight a few seconds late. Dixon makes a vicious swing at his target. Flipping out of the way, the guard kicks him in the jaw. Cartwheeling back he slices a four-inch wound in Dixon's back. He shouts in furious pain but quickly turns to face him. As he lunges back to the fight Jimmy slides in on the ground. In defence, the guard swings both hooked blades in an artistic circle. He catches Dixon's blade and yanks it from his hand. He misses a swing at Jimmy and receives a sliced ankle for it. His balance stumbling and one foe disarmed, he turns to face Jimmy.

Hearing the scream of the goliath behind him, the guard manages to curls around with grace and catch Dixon's prosthetic arm mid punch. Gripped by the hook blades at the wrist, Dixon grips the blades with his fake hand. Closing its robotic vice-like grip, the metal begins to bend. In a panic, the guard kicks Dixon's gut and pulls with all of his strength, severing the hand from the arm.

A corkscrew flip backwards and the guard is primed for a lunge at Dixon, who grips the wires flopping out of his stump. Before he reaches Dixon, a blade enters the guard's back. Jimmy whispers in his ear.

"Picked the wrong line of work, asshole". He kicks below where the blade entered his back as he yanks on the blade. Splitting the flesh open to reveal his spine the guard stumbles to Dixon. Grabbing him by the throat Dixon flails spit as he pants. Rage growing in him as his grip tightens, he screams at the guard, arching him into the air and slamming him into the ground so hard Jimmy feels like he lifts off the ground for a moment. A huge Calloway boot follows and stamps onto the guard's face. Jimmy recoils a little at the audible squish sound.

"Holy shit, Dix. I think you got him" Jimmy says, pulling back up beside his friend.

"They got Sadie," Dixon says as he looks down at his visceral work.

"What? I thought she was at her mother's?" asks Jimmy.

"They picked her up before she got away. Bastards slit her throat right in front of me" Dixon's rolling chest begins to calm.

"Damnit! Where are they now?"

"I got Yang. Fenghuang needs a new leader. Sutcliffe got away. We've got to get him before he ruins it all for everyone" Dixon turns to Jimmy.

"With no Yang, Sutcliffe will have an easier job of pushing through the merger. We've got to go" Jimmy says as they make their way to the door.

Entering the hallways of the compound they make their way down darkly red lit stretches. Matte black walls with little detail lead them to a set of lifts. They all open as they approach, ready to take a passenger on a journey. Dixon and Jimmy slide into the first one they get to, and look at the display.

"You think they'll have many people on the first floor, we're on basement level four right now," Jimmy asks.

"We're going to the top," Dixon says, plugging his thumb against the display. The doors close and a diagram of the building is displayed, with the lift cabin and the very top level highlighted.

"The top?" Jimmy falls back into the corner of the lift, catching his breath still.

"If Sutcliffe is still here, he'll be at the top. He'll have arrived at the top by shuttle as well. Either way our best chance of catching him is at the top." Dixon says. Jimmy is hit with a wave of realisation, he's right. There is no way Tom Sutcliffe would run out of the front door of any building even if the devil himself was chasing him.

Chapter 25

Stepping out at the top floor, the two flex ready for action. A gigantic black tiled floor greets them, not a soul is in sight. Large scarlet columns stretch down the length of the room on either side. The windows wide and tall, pillars of wall break them up with various pieces of historic war regalia in glass cabinets sitting in front of them. A mixture of Chinese and Japanese armour is posed in each one, with a couple of different weapons sitting below them. Polearms strap to the columns with vibrant coloured fabric dangling below the bladed ends. At the end of the room several red curtains hang, each with extensively detailed art depicting great armies in battle, huge cities under fire and mythical creatures descending from the skies.

"Hello?" Jimmy's voice echoes down the room and creeps back upon them. Dixon gives a disapproving look.

"What? At least there isn't any greeny this time" He smiles, Dixon smirks and shrugs. They walk the length of the grand hall-sized room, looking at the suits of armour. Posed in fighting stances, any one of them looking like it was ready to be possessed by a spirit and attack.

Dixon stretches his arm out, what was left of his second replacement arm at least. The flayed innards dangling out, he tries to gather up the loose pieces and clump them together, cramming them back into the prosthetic casing. Jimmy watches, raising his eyebrows in a silent bid to offer help.

"I got this" Dixon says, fumbling and repeatedly missing one artificial tendon as he tries to grab them all. Grunting in frustration he flings his arm, the pieces flailing wildly. Looking around he spots one of the samurai armour outfits, he pauses, raises an eyebrow and approaches.

"Uh, I think those might be quite expensive, maybe even historical antiques," Jimmy says as he watches Dixon smash one of the glass cases and rip the arm off a dummy. Rotating the arm as he investigates it, Dixon then rips the upper arm out of the armour sleeve. Gritting his teeth, he pulls violently at the Halo prosthetic. Jimmy squints as it looks almost like a man ripping flesh from his own body. The prosthetic removed with an audible tear, Dixon jams his stump into the armoured sleeve, tightening the bindings around his bicep and remaining elbow. He rolls his shoulder a few times, acclimatising to his now third arm.

"See, I told you I got this," Dixon says, pulling the arm up and adjusting the fingers with his real hand, leaving the mannequin's middle finger sticking up as Jimmy smirks.

Reaching the huge curtains, Jimmy sees that light shines through the narrow gaps between each one. Nudging past the curtains he finds Lady Yang's office. Nearly half the size of the hall, a desk hides in a shade similar to the black of the wall behind it. On the left, a large painting hangs of three horses almost leaping from the canvas. The rider on each horse looking dead ahead with an intent focus, one screams in the midst of throwing a spear, another aims a bow and arrow, and the final one swings a mace above his head. The plaque at the bottom reads "Caishen, King Yan and Guandi descend".

"You wouldn't think such a cold bitch would be so into her art, huh?" Jimmy says as Dixon follows through the curtains, looking out the windows and noticing the floor of clouds holding the spire up again.

"Makes me think of the four horsemen, doesn't seem as strange for her to be looking at the guys who'll bring about the end of days. Guess Sutcliffe got away in time" Dixon says approaching the desk. A computer display spins the Fenghuang logo in its centre. A large F interlaced with an H, nothing too flashy but instantly identifiable. Jimmy quickly moves around the desk to the chair, the red cushion hugging him into comfort. For a second he pauses in appreciation before Dixon slaps his shoulder. He begins tapping away at the keyboard. The logo disappears and several stacks with corporate designations fly up.

"Give me a second" Jimmy says, pulling his arm display up and interfacing it with the computer. The green of his arm occasionally gradating red, the small Leistung logo in his display flickering, not knowing which logo to display. He twitches violently, gripping his arm as the shock singes the hairs on it.

"You ok?" asks Dixon.

"I'm good, they've got some nasty protection on this computer." He rattles away on the keyboard some more and a couple of the stacks of files disappear. Zooming in on one of them Jimmy smiles.

"I've got her personal files here, let's see. Schedule, business contacts, personal emails. Ah ha! Got it, her login for her shuttle." Jimmy says as a buzzing can be faintly heard. One of the windows parts from its frame and slides upwards. As it does so, a platform approaches, creeping out from a floor below and moving up to the open window. Resting on the platform sits a black shuttle, different to the previous shuttle they had encountered, this one gleamed a shining red. Black stripes frame its outline and a darker red forms an understated logo.

Dixon looks it up and down, clearly designed for a smooth fast ride, he is excited to get into it. A little luxury is always nice when hunting down the man who killed your ex-wife. He turns to Jimmy and motions him to join.

"Wow, wait a second" Jimmy's eyes nearly explode as he looks at the display. A mixture of video and documents displaying in unison. "Dixon, look at this". Dixon runs over and Jimmy restarts the video and pushes the volume up. A woman's face shows on the display while she adjusts the camera she is recording with.

"Hello, my name is Abena Boro," she says in a charming African accent.

"Hey, she's the girl who discovered the GID, right?" Dixon asks, Jimmy nods.

"I am currently working at the Halo research lab in Massachusetts, I've discovered what I think is something quite interesting." Her face lighting up with excitement. "My team and I have found a hidden gene within human DNA. Our tests are still in the early stages but its potential seems quite astounding. If we are correct, we may be able to make a huge leap forward in medicine." The display cuts to static and then back to another recording, Jimmy fast forwards through a few videos of Abena, gaining excitement and flashing a bigger and bigger smile each time.

"Medicine? GIDs are basically nature's guidance councillor" Dixon says, confused. Jimmy plays the last video on the file.

"It's been two years. We've finished the majority of our tests and sent the results up to Halo top brass." Faint discussion can be heard in the background, some of it happy, some of it cautious and mixed with hushed tones. "We've been told from management that we are receiving full funding to take this further. We'll all have bigger salaries and be able to get more specialised equipment…" She leans in closer to the camera as she looks back, checking that her staff are still talking amongst themselves and not listening in.

"The thing is, I also caught wind that they don't want to use the gene how we've intended. Those marketing poison tongues have got to Tom Sutcliffe and convinced him that they can rebrand it as a predictor of people's potential." She furrows her brow. "I've never heard of anything so ridiculous in my life. We've found a way to predict with almost supernatural accuracy any hereditary diseases. Hell, from that alone we've managed to pull out cures for three different cancers. This gene is like a recipe book for medicine. Now they want to lock it all up and call it something else?" Her voice grows louder, one of her staff notices. Abena turns to her as she approaches and begins to chat, the video cuts. Jimmy turns to Dixon with an expression of pure surprise.

"What? She found a…"Dixon cuts himself off, the two of them looking off into space in shock.

"What happened to her?" Dixon asks. Jimmy slowly turns back to the file and skims through the document.

"She was removed from the facility for 'debriefing' and the team was disbanded throughout the globe. They'll probably all be dead by now though, I'd assume", says Jimmy.

Dixon's eyes sift through space as he thinks. "Grab those files, we're going to need them. We're taking the shuttle, you think you can get a track on where Sutcliffe might have gone?"

"Yang had his contact details, we can get tracking from that". Jimmy says, pulling the contact details from the display in his arm. They run to the shuttle, Jimmy taps on his arm and the doors part like a mouth opening. Sitting down inside Dixon looks at the pilot seat.

"You know how to fly this thing?"

"Don't need to, I can set the autopilot for it. We'll coast along in the clouds to Halo HQ. Nobody will spot us until we're stepping out of this thing". Jimmy says, flicking data from his arm to the console display in the cockpit. He shows his arm to Dixon. A beacon highlights on a map of the city, positioned over the Halo headquarters a small tag springs off of it. "Tom Sutcliffe – Halo CEO".

Chapter 26

Stealthily soaring across the sky, hidden in a cloud of concealment, Dixon tightens the bindings on his arm and admires the craftsmanship. A black gauntlet with inlays of gold, all of it wrapping around the gauntlet in a tapestry of cherry blossom trees. He shakes his head, doing his best to laugh at the irony.

"Want another replacement?" Jimmy asks.

"As long as it isn't anything from Halo" Dixon chuckles.

"Two hands lost in a week. That's got to be an achievement." Says Jimmy.

"At least I didn't feel this one get chopped off" he rotates the arm a few times as they both look at it. "Maybe I should get a matching samurai arm on the other side?" He laughs, Jimmy remains quiet.

"Hey, Dix, I'm sorry about Sadie. This has all gone shit-stack sideways. I know you probably don't want to talk about it, but I just want you to know I'm here for you, buddy" Jimmy says turning a serious tone.

"I know, man. I may not always be one to open up much but, you know, thanks. You were there for me when Rose and Jenny died. You've always been there to help, even when I lost RJ." He raises his stump with a sarcastic smile. "Sadie was an amazing woman, I loved her, I mean, I love her. I don't think I've really ever talked about it with anyone else but her. She was my life, the kids were my life. They are all gone now." Tears begin to well up in Dixon's eyes, though his face is still locked in its focus. "I guess I'm slightly happy for her, she's with them now. Sounds kind of corny I know. I didn't realise how much it hit her, think I was too caught up in my own problems to notice." He wipes the tears as they run down his cheek, looks at his wet fingers, grimaces at Jimmy and shows his hand.

"You ever think you'd see me cry?" Dixon asks.

Jimmy smiles "Hey, you lost your arm twice and I've seen you cry - all in the same week. It's definitely an achievement now." Dixon laughs through more tears.

"I know you hold that shit back from people, bury it deep down inside and hide your weaknesses, I get that. You don't need to hide anything from me though." Jimmy reassures.

"I've only got one thing left to do." Dixon looks out the front window, the outline of their destination slowly growing as they get closer. "Kill the man who killed Sadie."

Jimmy looks to the floor, almost welling up at the respect and appreciation Dixon showed to him. "We will, buddy, we will". Dixon nods to his best friend. They sit in silence, both feeling closer to their friend than ever, both focussing on the task at hand.

The Halo headquarters building looms over them as they approach, still hiding in the clouds. It's epic size almost feeling like a cunning creature waiting for them to enter its trap. They begin to ascend, carefully flying up a corner of the building with fewer windows than anywhere else. Reaching the top they see the landing pad they had arrived at previously.

"Look! That must be his shuttle." Jimmy points down to a shuttle parked slightly askew on the landing pad, its doors still open.

"I guess he was in a bit of a panic when he arrived. Let's go and give him a reason to panic." Dixon says. The shuttle circles above the building before diving down, turning up sharply before it reaches the landing pad, dust blowing up from the surface. The landing gear softly touches down. Jimmy shuts off the engine and the doors open.

Dixon and Jimmy enter through the same impressive door. People sit in the bar area just like before, if slightly less of them. A few of them rise, clearly reading the situation - they fluster. Two of them quickly approach.

"You can't be here, Tom doesn't want you filthy..." before they can finish Dixon's hand grips tightly around one of their throats, slamming the man into the ground. Jimmy plants a pinpoint perfect punch directly to the others face, knocking him out flat. The rest of the people scurry for the lifts as the two fierce-looking men walk closer. A few scramble for the staircase door as the lifts slowly ascend. Looking over to the bar, the bartender looks back awkwardly, feigning a welcoming smile and looking at the only patron sitting drinking.

Tom Sutcliffe sits on a bar stool, swirling a glass with a dark spirit in it. His hair dishevelled from anxious hands running through it. His posture nervous and twitchy. He doesn't hear the panicked mass trying to escape.

"Sutcliffe!" Dixon shouts, his voice booming around the room and making some people duck, Tom turns his head slightly, unsure if he actually heard the voice or if it was his imagination. Seeing the two figures approach he flaps, accidentally sending his drink to the ground. It smashes, but Tom's attention is now focused on also escaping his foes. He launches from the bar stool and bolts up the staircase. Jimmy and Dixon give chase, reaching the top of the stairs they see him fly into his office, adjacent to the conference room they'd all spoke in before. The glass windows suddenly going opaque as Tom presses a button at his desk.

Dixon wastes no time in charging the door. Shouting violently as he throws his club like foot at it. The door crunches and flies off one of its hinges as he coasts into the room. Jimmy follows behind him only to see Dixon turn to face Tom's desk. A bullet sails through Dixon's shoulder, puckering flesh and blood out of his back. Dixon barks in pain as he stumbles towards the desk. Tom begins to lower the gun as Jimmy makes a straight line for him. Leaping over the desk Jimmy kicks at Tom's hands, too quickly for Tom to turn the gun on him.

Applying his muscle memory training, he quickly circles Tom, taking an arm behind him and thrusting it up into the middle of his back. Tom screams as he is forced face down into his desk. Nearly knocking him out, Jimmy grips the back of Tom's head and looks to Dixon.

"Dixon, you alright?" He shouts.

Dixon rises from his knees, pawing at the wound in his shoulder. His hand stained red with blood, he reaches to the exit wound in his back. He hisses at the stinging from the hole, but reassures Jimmy with a nod. He approaches the desk, places his hand where Jimmy was holding Tom's head. Jimmy steps aside.

"Hello again, Tom!" Dixon throws him back against the wall, pushing the chair out of the way. As he bounces back he is met be a series of almighty punches to the head and torso, each one bouncing him back off the wall. Tom finally manages to muster some strength and attempts to throw a punch at Dixon. He sidesteps easily, grabbing the thrown fist as he elbows Tom's face back to the desk, reeling his arm back in a direction it shouldn't go until a disgusting crack can be heard.

"So glad to see you again, we didn't quite get to finish things off did we? You left so quickly, that's quite rude, you know?" Dixon yanks the broken arm sending Tom to the ground, sitting against the wall he'd been ping-ponged off moments before.

"We had to come and have a chat with you, get some closure after you killed Sadie" Dixon kneels at Tom's side, the beaten man's breathing erratic and anxious. "We stumbled across something most interesting while we were trying to chase you down though." Dixon stands, motions over Jimmy.

Jimmy sits on the desk facing Tom, bringing up his arm display, he quickly flicks up the video of Abena Boro. Her voice cutting deep into Tom, almost hurting him more than the broken arm and beating he was suffering from.

"Where did you get that?" he asks frantically.

"Your good pal Myra Yang had it locked away in her system." Jimmy says, "Guess she did a little bit of digging in your database. Any good CEO should really do a background check on any company they decide to merge with, don't you think?"

"The real question is, how long have you known about this, huh?" Dixon lightly slaps Tom on the face, gaining his attention again. "Bet you've been sitting on that for a while."

Tom shrinks into himself and slowly begins to whimper softly. "My grandfather..." Dixon looks to Jimmy, he shrugs.

"He started this company, built it into a scientific leader in the industry. He was ruthless in his work though. A businessman heading a company full of scientists. Throwing blank cheques at each and every one of them until someone came through with something." Snot drips from his nose as he sobs.

"He nearly bankrupted the entire organisation. When he found out about Boro's work he took it over and warped it into a cash cow. I don't think he could have even predicted that it would literally change the world." He raises his head. "Why does that matter, when you're rich beyond dreams though?"

"Your grandfather buried the truth, I'm guessing your father had the same cold heart and so do you?" Dixon prods at his chest, Tom shakes his head and waves his hands.

"No, no. My father tried to make things right. He knew that using the research to create cures was the right thing to do. He couldn't come clean about it all though. That would sink the company overnight. Everyone that worked for us would lose their jobs, millions worldwide would be homeless. We wouldn't have any way to stop someone else from stealing it all from under us and taking over everything." His brow wrinkled as he explains.

"He put together a plan to bring together some of the most powerful people in the world, and make them work in unison to provide this miracle to people. We'd save everyone." He smiles faintly.

Jimmy looks to Dixon confused. "Wait, your father tried to reveal the truth. What stopped him?"

Tom ironically chuckles. "That's the kicker, we could have made a cure for cancer. If only he hadn't died of it, he might have been able to achieve his goal."

Dixon sneers, grabbing Tom by the scruff of his suit jacket, lifting him up to his feet then pressing him against the wall.

"There's just one thing I don't understand." he says as Jimmy panics behind him.

"Dixon, hold on a sec" Jimmy halts him, unsure of his next steps.

Dixon looks deep into Tom's eyes. "If you're trying to complete your dad's goody too shoes plan to make things right. Why are you making people slaves? Why carry out your father's merger plan and make one company dictate our futures? That bullshit about making a giant slave workforce to help fix problems, that all part of the plan as well? Or was that some marketing crap you made up too?"

Tom curls a smile at the edges of his mouth. "Well, my father never finished his plan for one reason…" A light ding can be heard across the floor. The doors of the two lifts at the lower level open, Halo guards flood the bar area, empty now from all the fearful elite in their mass exodus. They march up the stairs and stand facing Tom's office, their weapons drawn and focused.

"He was too weak!" Tom whispers, kicking off the wall and pushing Dixon back. They tumble over each other. Tom quickly scrambles to the desk and hits a button, the windows turning transparent again. The guards spot Tom and Dixon, they stare back staggered.

"Fire!" Tom shouts as he throws himself behind an extravagant looking metal chair. Jimmy reacts with speed, flipping the desk over and pulling Dixon behind it. The guard's gunfire rips through the windows and sends pieces of glass and material darting around the room, shattering the back window. A gust of wind from outside sucks out a small coffee table and some debris. After a few moments, the fire stops.

"Come out with your hands in the air" a guard's voice shouts.

"Suck a dick" Dixon shouts, looking around the room until he sees Tom hiding behind a chair. He quickly throws himself to the chair, clutching Tom and putting him in a chokehold in front of himself as he stands from the chair. The guards aim at the two of them as he holds Tom tightly.

"Dixon, what the hell are you doing?" Jimmy shouts from behind the desk.

"Stay there, Jimmy." Dixon looks over to his friend, seeing the dread on his face.

"This is your plan?" Tom snickers, while Dixon's one remaining real arm clenches around his neck. "Take me hostage?"

"Not exactly, I'd been mulling over a few different ways to kill you on the way over," Dixon says, looking over to Jimmy again. "Still got the files?" Jimmy nods. "Good, see if you can get them out to as many people as possible from Tom's computer". Jimmy looks at the computer, tumbled from the desk and lying on its side next to him.

"Guards, you serve me and this company" Tom begins to speak. Dixon leans into his ear.

"That's right. We're putting the truth out. Give it to the whole world and let them decide what to do with it. Not some spoilt billionaire."

"If you want to save your jobs, your lives, the world. I command you to shoot right now!" Tom screams at his guards.

"Dixon, you've got to move" Jimmy begs.

Dixon looks across and smiles calmly. "No Jimmy, I need to be here. I lost my daughters to a rich man who thought he could play how he likes. I lost my wife to this rich man who thinks he can play the world how he likes. Well, now I'm going to show them this isn't a game."

"FIRE!" Tom shouts. A couple of guards stutter as three unload their weapons at Tom and Dixon, both of them flinching as each bullet pierces through their bodies. Jimmy screams as he watches. Dixon still looking over at his friend can't hear his screams, instead, everything seems to move in slow motion. The two of them step backwards as they are pushed back by gunfire.

Blood drips on the carpet as they reach the edge of the window sill. Dixon looks into his friend's eyes as he feels the cooling breeze of the air, so cold up here that he finds it refreshing compared to the warmth building in his bullet-ridden chest. Dixon steps back and smiles at Jimmy, the man who had done everything he could to help him. He would miss him.

Chapter 27

Jimmy gawked at the empty window in silence, where his best friend had just been standing. Blinking a couple of times hoping his vision would correct itself or he'd wake up from this nightmare. The gunfire stopped, the guards also look at the window, taken aback at the order to shoot at their boss. Some surprised that they had witnessed their colleagues execute such an order, and the others surprised further that they had actually executed it.

Jimmy curls his head into his hands, holding back the tears he anticipates. Too shaken even to cry for his friend he wipes his face. Desperately trying to grab onto some train of thought in his now empty, head he remembers Dixon's request. Grabbing the computer, he quickly sets to, transferring the videos to the computer and making a CEO level announcement. Every screen in the building, including the exterior marketing screens, flickers to display the video. Jimmy then sends the video out to as many media channels as possible, and sets the building's security to public, allowing anyone in the region to tap into the broadcast.

The guards turn from the empty window and whistle of the passing wind, to the screen across the room which blinks to life.

Abena Boro's face repeating the words that Jimmy and Dixon had heard only hours before.

Chapter 28

"Hope you're happy now," Tom says as he hurtles towards the earth next to Dixon. Their wounds sending a spray into the skies above them, blood chasing them to the ground.

"We're both going to die," Tom says, his voice muffled a little by the descent.

"Yup," Dixon says, a broad smile on his face.

"All you're doing is making a martyr of me you realise" Tom smiles back, trying to wipe Dixon's away.

"Think again," Dixon says as the giant external screen of the building flickers to show Abena's face. Tom screams at the screen, trying to punch it as the fly down past it, feeling like they take forever to go by its giant size.

"Bit hard to be a martyr if everyone knows you're a liar" Dixon shouts over the screams.

"So what? You win? You're still going to die!" Tom says after trying to compose himself in impending doom.

"Yup, that's a good thing though. I'm done with this world, done hurting, done hating, done holding people back." Dixon looks down at the city as it grows closer.

Tom searches for something to say, a reasoning, a comeback, an insult. Nothing comes to mind, nor did it matter. Nothing could change the fact that he was looking at his end race towards him. A building that scoffed at him. His last act to scream in terror as he is splattered into the roof, his body turning to a pulp and smearing some windows.

Dixon misses the building and keeps falling, seeing all the different displays showing the videos of Boro. Jimmy hadn't failed him, he'd saved him. He thought about all the times he'd heard people talk about your life flashing before your eyes before you die. He never really believed in any of that touchy-feely crap. On the brink of his end, he couldn't help but look back on his years.

Working all those shifts with a man he never thought he would like. A cheeky little fellow, who despite his handsome looks couldn't seem to hold a relationship down. The man who had stood by him regardless of whether he agreed or not with Dixon's motivations. A man who put everything on the line to help him, even if it was just to make his friend feel a little happier. Dixon felt sorry for all the times he'd told Jimmy to stay back and work with him. Maybe it had just been so that Dixon could get help with the pencil pushing, maybe it was so that Jimmy could become the amazing cop he was today. Maybe doing that was why Jimmy struggled to keep a significant other. He wanted him to know he couldn't have pulled off anything without him. Wanted Jimmy to know that he never meant to hold him back from getting the wife and kids he always wanted.

Dixon's mind drifted to his own kids. His two daughters faces looking up at him from the breakfast table, smiling at him as he kissed them goodbye to leave for work. Their first days of school, hugging him close as he reassured them that everything was going to be alright. Opening presents on Christmas day and seeing them spellbound at the idea of Santa Claus bringing them the toy they'd been desperate for. Watching them play in the ocean as he looked on from the beach with Sadie.

His heartwarming visions of seeing Sadie for the first time flooded his head. The way time seemed to stop as he saw her, he may have put on a tough exterior to hide his truth but he was always a romantic deep inside. The only person to really make him weak, and make him want to be weak around her. The way she tied her hair back when she tried to focus on something. Her frustration at Dixon when he'd forget to pick up something on the way home. Her quick wit as she'd forgive him with playful teasing. The moment she made him the happiest man alive by saying yes. When she'd told him that she loved him all this time even though he'd destroyed himself mentally and physically.

The people he loved in this world had loved him regardless of what he put himself through or what he put them through. He smiled at the thought of being so lucky to have such people in his life. Feeling a well of pain as he knew that he would have laid his life on the line for them at any request. Hopefully, with his last act, he could be redeemed for any hurt he'd caused. And with that, he ended.

Only a few people in the street reacted to the body colliding with the pavement in front of them. Most eyes were fixated on the displays.

Chapter 29

Jimmy pokes his head out from behind the table, none of the guards face his direction. All stare at the screens, their helmets removed and their faces stunned as the entire city hears the revelation and deceit. Jimmy slowly walks out of the room and cautiously slides up beside one of the guards, his gun leaning against the rail of the staircase. Another guard sees Jimmy, flinches and points his gun, blinks a few times and then lowers his aim and looks back at the screen.

"What does this mean for us now?" The guard nearest to Jimmy asks, not looking his way.

"It means we have a new world to build." He says watching the video as it loops from the last one to first.

"Are we going to be ok?" the guard turns to Jimmy, his face questioning and scared.

Jimmy turns to the guard, takes a large breath while looking at the ground, looks into his eyes and says. "We should be fine" he nods, patting the guard on the arm and makes his way down to the lift.

As he exits the building, Jimmy sees the extent of his work. Expecting that there would be a bit of surprise in the Halo staff, but seeing the public pause to take in the information, made the city appear like someone had stopped time.

The cold wind brushing on his face, he zips his jacket closed, shoves his hands into his pockets and begins to walk through the crowd of living statues all looking up.

Chapter 30

Three weeks have passed and Jimmy still thinks back to that day. Today more so than ever as he stands at the grave of Dixon Callaway. A gravestone that Dixon might have approved of, Jimmy suspected his friend wouldn't want anyone to bother with a funeral for him. It wasn't a large fancy tombstone, but one placed next to his family. His daughters' graves still covered in the moss and growth of years of nature. Dixon's grave sits next to them, clean and proud. Sadie's grave on the other side of the girls. A family together again.

Jimmy can't cry for his friend, he still sees him. Looking back at him with his playful disdain for Jimmy's wisecracking. The colourful insults and jabs at each other. He'd always looked up to Dixon when they worked together. He'd made him a better man, he knew that all the ribbing and roughhousing was Dixon's way of showing his best friend he cared about him. He wanted to thank Dixon for all the years of service he'd given to the city, for all the days where he didn't know he'd raised Jimmy's spirit. He didn't want to go home to his empty apartment and drink himself to sleep. Helping Dixon complete all that paperwork was therapy to him, therapy that only built a stronger bond between him and his partner, his friend. When Dixon broke and became and turned inwards there was no question that Jimmy knew he had to help him. He wouldn't be the man he was today without him, how could he let him rot at the bottom of a bottle.

Jimmy smiles, looking across the gravestones, thinking how much Sadie would be overjoyed at being with her girls again. How much of a hard time she would give Dixon, trying to make him admit how beautiful it was. The girls had their parents back, he swallows back the emotion in his throat as fingers interlace his right hand.

Maria Sorensen smiles politely as Jimmy looks up to her. Her hair tied back and sitting under a black hat, she stands with Jimmy. Looking over the graves she lightly wraps her arms around Jimmy's.

"You did it, Dix," Jimmy says to the cold stone standing from the ground. "You saved us all. I hope you're happy now, you big schmuk." He laughs a little as the tears come through. Maria leans her head on his shoulder, shedding a couple of tears herself.

"Gonna miss you, buddy. Tell the girls I'm asking for them." He smiles and wipes his cheeks. Turning to Maria he nods and they walk out of the cemetery. The warm sunlight hugging them close as they leave.

Jimmy had finally managed to muster up the courage to ask Maria out for a coffee. With everything that had happened, she'd gladly accepted, and after she turned up to their meeting in a stunningly elegant dress, Jimmy realised she wasn't just wanting to debrief. She'd made the mischievous remark that she thought he would have turned up in a suit for a date. Jimmy blushed as she said the word date, and by the end of the night, the two couldn't be stopped from enjoying each other's conversation.

The majority of high-level executives had been dethroned. A few of them still surviving in their positions due to their friendlier dispositions and evident qualifications for their roles. The rest fending for themselves in a world where everyone of a lower class had worked hard to learn their crafts and figure out how to exist.

The lowest levels had found so many new opportunities and acceptance that small businesses began to pop up on most street corners. Shops, barbers, supermarkets catering to a wide range of goods all being sourced locally. Communities no longer bunched together, trying to hide from one another, but looked to their neighbours for help and to assist. Suicide rates began to drop, drug offenders found it easier to find assistance. Crime was still prevalent in poverty-stricken areas, but to a lesser degree. Thieves and con artists were the most common criminals seen on corners now, no longer gang bangers and rapists. People no longer stood under the banner of the Halo flag, and there were whispers of the words "America" again. This time unlike all those politicians from history, the country really had been given back to the people.

They didn't want to argue and steal and hurt each other. They wanted to grow, to accept, to learn. The technologies around them had been expensive and unattainable. Now, without the fear of dying at every opportunity, they could build their own neighbourhoods into a pleasant place to live. They could joke and laugh and smile. The police were even accepted as a welcome sight around the streets. "Protect and serve" was once again respected instead of the fear of "dictate and intimidate".

Jimmy had been accepted by his fellow detectives and was promoted. When he walked around the precinct, people stopped to listen to him now. Even his funny stories of debauchery from years past were popular for his peers to hear.

Guys he'd never met would offer to grab him a coffee in the morning. He would be asked for opinions on cases, and when he gave his take, people were impressed at his vision.

There were rumours around the precinct that Jimmy had been offered chief of police but had turned it down. The idea amused Jimmy so much, he corrected anyone he overheard talking about it. Still, the change in his life's tone was all too welcome.

He sits down at his desk, a smallish pile of documents sitting at his table. Jimmy now requested that his cases be delivered to him in paper format. A gentle reminder of how he had got to this point. If it hadn't been for Dixon's primal rage and keen eyes they wouldn't have stumbled across the undisclosed attempt to destroy their lives. A young cadet pokes his head into Jimmy's office, knocking on the frame of the door.

"Detective Kershon?" the voice calm and respectful, Jimmy still wasn't quite used to people actually calling him by his title.

"Yes, cadet. What can I do for you?" He says, looking up from his scribblings.

The young man enters the room and stands to attention in front of the desk. "Captain has requested your presence, sir!"

"Very good, thank you, cadet." Jimmy stands as the cadet salutes him, he could only remember being saluted twice in his life. Once when he was sworn into the force, and when he received his promotion a week ago. Was this something he'd have to get used to? The two leave the office, the cadet returning down the stairs to his station. Jimmy turns in the other direction and walks into his captain's office. A large room walled with glass, his captain sits behind the desk focused on taking notes and ignoring as many calls as possible.

"Kershon! Glad you could make it" he smiles playfully.

"You don't need to send one of the rookie's to get me, cap. My office is fifteen feet from you, you could shout and I'll come running." Jimmy says, standing in front of the desk in a stance not too dissimilar to the cadets at Jimmy's desk. The captain looks him up and down and smiles again.

"At ease, detective" he chuckles, standing from his desk. "I know it might seem a little pompous but it's always good to be respected." Jimmy curls his mouth a little, thankful for his captain's vague compliment. "It's also good for the rest of the precincts morale to have a hero among them, someone to look up to." Jimmy can't hide his grin, nodding a thank you to him.

"The reason I have you here though, detective Kershon, is that I have a case for you." The captain brings his arm up, the holo-display glinting for a moment, Jimmy has to concentrate on it for a second and not look in awe at the decorated chest of his superior.

"Yes, sir, what's the case" his concentration drawn to the subject. He'd never been offered a case in this fashion.

"There's been three murders, two suspects, they have owned up to two of the murders respectively. Neither of them is taking the blame for the third death. Thing is, all of the murders fit the exact same MO. I want you to head up the investigation". The captain taps his arm and Jimmy's arm lights up in turn, the information transferred successfully.

"Right away, sir" Jimmy smiles, nods and exits the room. As he crosses the bull pit, the captain shouts from his doorway.

"Oh, and Kershon?" he watches as Jimmy turns to face him, eyebrows raised.

"I've got a new partner for you".